Lifted!

Vanessa G. Cunningham, M.A., J.D.

CHICAGO SPECTRUM PRESS
LOUISVILLE, KY 40207

© 2002 by Vanessa G. Cunningham

All Scripture quotations are taken from *The Holy Bible*
The King James Study Bible (KJV) - *The Book of Job*
©1988 by Liberty University

Cover design by Dorothy Kavka

For copies, questions or comments contact
the author at:
    Lifted! Ministries, Inc.
    P.O. Box 221255
    Louisville, KY 40252-1255
    1.877.BLifted (1.877.254.3833)
    e-mail: IBnLifted@aol.com
    webpage: www.BLifted.com

the publisher at:
    Chicago Spectrum Press
    4824 Brownsboro Center
    Louisville, KY 40207
    1.800.594.5190
    e-mail: EvanstonPB@aol.com
    webpage: www.EvanstonPublishing.com

Printed in the U.S.A.

10 9 8 7 6 5 4 3 2 1

ISBN: 1-58374-048-1

Table of Contents

PART I: ECZEMA

PART II: ABUSE

Acknowledgments

I thank God for making it possible for me to communicate the messages that these pages convey.

I also thank Dr. Maya Angelou, who inspired me through her book, *I Know Why The Caged Bird Sings*, to put into written words what my heart and soul were quenching.

Thank you also to Dr. Sena Jeter Naslund, my thesis director, who was the impetus behind this great project taking form, and to Dr. Robert L. Douglas and Dr. Karen Chandler, my thesis committee readers—all from the University of Louisville.

Special gratitude to my son, Christopher, who gave me space to write, to my lifelong friends, Blanche, Clyde, Cynthia, Deborah, Donna, John, Joyce, Judith, Kay, Phillip (a.k.a. "P.J."), Sherree', Toni, and Yalonda, who were my early readers and supporters, and whose encouragement, confidence and enthusiasm spurred me to fulfill this mission.

Last, but certainly not least of all, thank you to my mother and father (Elnora and Doris), and to my sisters (Yvonne and Hermena) and brothers (Stanley and Anthony), who individually and collectively have played a major role in my development and success.

Preface

Dear Reader,

The caterpillar appears to slowly crawl on its belly. It then forms a cocoon, a hard shell casing. While inside the cocoon the caterpillar undergoes a transformation from an unsightly, squirmy, hairy, worm-like creature into a beautiful butterfly.

Like the caterpillar, whose life is abased until it completes its metamorphic cycle into a winged creature that can flap its wings and fly, so is the life of Vonnette Covington, the protagonist in *Lifted!*

Vonnette is a young woman who is repeatedly ostracized and victimized by those whom she feels closest to.

Resembling the life-phases of the caterpillar, Vonnette undergoes a conversion. She seeks shelter and refuge in the Church from the emotional and physical pains that plague her. The Church becomes Vonnette's protective enclosure.

Akin to the lowly caterpillar, which is afterward transformed into a striking creature, Vonnette triumphs over trauma through her impregnable self-will and determination and shows forth God's "good" creation. And, while remaining steadfast in *The Book of Job*, by faith in God, she is *Lifted!*

My purpose for writing this inspirational prose is to be a voice for those who, like Vonnette, have been victimized, abused, and misused. My hope is that the Vonnette's of the world will exit their cocoons and get help from their hurts. This book is intended to be a blessing and an encouragement for the silent wounded—to bring healing, deliverance, repentance, and forgiveness.

To my son, Christopher.

And—

For all those whose wings
are too weary to
flap and take flight—
May you read this and soar.

PART I

ECZEMA

Vanessa G. Cunningham

CHAPTER I

SCALY SKIN

I found comfort in the book of Job after suffering many years with a gruesome skin disease called eczema, which covered at least 90% of my body. I was in elementary school when this condition began to develop. My skin would itch terribly—particularly in the fold of my arms, behind my knees, and the back of my neck— especially when I got upset. Oh, I'd have itching tantrums. I cut my nails to prevent myself from further bruising my skin until it would bleed, but when I could no longer resist, I'd get a sharp comb or a hard-bristled brush and scratch with it until I was soothed:

> *So went Satan forth from the presence of the Lord, and smote Job with sore boils from the sole of his foot unto his crown. And he took him a potsherd to scrape himself withal; and he sat down among the ashes. (Job 2:7-8).*

When my sister and I slept together, due to lack of space, she kicked and pinched me during the night when I scratched. She hated the noisome, bothersome sandpaper sound.

"Mommy, make Vonnette stop scratching!" she'd yell from the top of her lungs.

"Stop scratching, Vonnette," my mother retorted harshly from her bedroom.

In the morning when I arose I scraped the sheet of the scaly, dry, dead skin that had fallen off during the night. Then I'd sweep up the skin with a dustpan and broom.

> *When I lie down, I say, When shall I arise, and the night be gone? And I am full of tossings to and fro unto the dawning of the day. (Job 7:4).*

လလလလလလလ

For years my parents took me to specialists and dermatologists throughout the city to help me. But the doctors only wrote prescriptions for topical ointments, said it was chronic eczema, and sent us on our way. They said I would have it all my life and there was no cure for it. They ran all kinds of allergy tests on me and told me what foods, animals and trees to avoid—none of which seemed to help, because the rash just continued to spread. Eventually, my feet were the only place on my body that the rash did not invade. I loved my feet.

৯৯৯৯৯৯৯

My family lived on the fifteenth floor in the projects in Harlem—not far from the Apollo. I had two sisters, Gayle and Wilhelmina—both older than me, and two brothers, Ulysses and Dwayne—one older and one younger. My sisters and I shared the back bedroom, my two brothers shared the middle one, and my parents had the first bedroom, which was closest to the bathroom.

৯৯৯৯৯৯৯

Our family wasn't considered poor—at least not in our eyes, although for a short while we were receiving government powdered milk, eggs, and potatoes, which occupied a spot atop our white cabinets collecting grease and dust. We hated the imitation, artificial taste, and only resorted to its ingestion during extreme hunger.

We were also rationed a long, pale-orange rectangular block of delicious American cheese that didn't last until our next supply, and a brick of whitish-yellow butter that was so difficult to penetrate that we struggled, seemingly forever, to sink our knife into. Most of the time, to avoid being late to school, we passed up toast with butter and used jelly only.

We also received an allotment of stick-to-the-roof-of-your-mouth-and-suffocate peanut butter in the can topped with oil. After placing a knife or spoon into the peanut butter we could turn the can upside down and play catch with it; neither the spoon nor the peanut butter would be displaced. You could build your muscles trying to stir it, tear your bread into shreds while attempting to spread it on thinly, and asphyxiate from putting too much in your mouth.

CHAPTER II

DISOWNED

I didn't feel my mother was supportive at all when she allowed my sisters and brothers to pick on me and laugh at me along with other people. After what seemed like hours of misery, Mommy calmly said, "Leave Vonnette alone." It was too late.

Sometimes Wilhelmina, who was just a year older than I, and Dwayne, my younger brother, disowned me. They would say, "She's not my sister," out in public, because they were embarrassed by my appearance. This cut me to the core of my soul, humiliated me, and made me feel insecure and unloved. But I would go on loving and forgiving them—even when they couldn't care less if I forgave them or not.

> *All my inward friends abhorred me: and they whom I loved are turned against me. My bone cleaveth to my skin and to my flesh, and I am escaped with the skin of my teeth. (Job 19:19-20).*

Generally, Ulysses and Gayle sheltered me from harassment when they were around, and would plead with Wilhelmina to leave me alone; but she didn't. She found pleasure in my anguish. Dwayne was often just around for the laughs. He hardly initiated strife.

Our parents never allowed us to use foul language. We couldn't even say the word "lie." We had to say, "He told a story," or "She's not telling the truth." And we had better not use the word "hate." That was absolutely forbidden. They said we didn't know enough to hate anything or anybody; but not everyone obeyed the rules. Wilhelmina, with whom I slept, would sneak and slyly tell me, "I hate you," whenever she took a notion. She would roll her eyes and cut through me like a sharp bolt of electricity. She meant it. I'd better not tell—or else.

> *For the thing which I greatly feared is come upon me, and that which I was afraid of is come unto me. I was not in safety, neither had I rest, neither was I quiet; yet trouble came. (Job 3:25-26).*

Lifted!

When one of us got in trouble, Daddy would be the one to whip us most of the time. As soon as Daddy arrived home from work Mommy gave him a report. Daddy had two whipping belts, a broken-in one-and-one-half-inch wide thick brown one, with a buckle, and a three-quarter-inch wide thin one, without a buckle. The thin one was usually in our parents' bedroom drawer; Daddy wore the thick one in his pants. It seemed the thin one hurt more; nevertheless, it was best to avoid them both.

જ&જ&જ&જ&જ&

We always hated for Daddy to come home from work when we knew we were in trouble; but once he did, we wanted to get our beating over with because we had already been scoffed by our siblings and tortured with thoughts of painful whelps and bruises. Whatever we did to deserve the whipping, we hardly repeated our mistakes.

Rarely would we get out of line in the playground in front of our building, because although our parents may not have been downstairs watching us, the neighbors were. We were taught to "obey those that had the rule over us,"—which meant all adults. The neighbors would wring our necks for our parents first, tell on us, and then we were subjected to a double portion of our parents' wrath for embarrassing them in public.

CHAPTER III

THE FIGHTS

Daddy called me a "mummy" once when he was drunk, but I knew it was really Smirnoff talking. He loved me. I felt his love. He often hugged me and told me so.

Nearly every Friday night, on payday, Daddy came home late from gambling, reeking of Pall Mall cigarettes and Vodka. The scent made the whole apartment malodorous. He and Mommy argued at the top of their lungs. I hated when they fought. Surely the neighbors were getting an earful listening through the walls or under the door (as we did when we heard them fighting and arguing).

Practically every Friday night, like clockwork, our parents would awaken my sisters, brothers and me. At times we didn't even go to sleep. We would just lie there, waiting for the expected. Occasionally, we'd creep out of our beds and tiptoe to the kitchen or living room to make sure they weren't killing each other.

"Go to bed," they yelled shooing us away, as if all was peaceful. Ulysses made the rest of us stand back while he intervened during their altercations. In a strong stern voice he'd say, "Why don't you all stop! Don't do this! You're upsetting everybody!"

> *I would seek unto God, and unto God would I commit my cause: Which doeth great things and unsearchable; marvelous things without number: Who giveth rain upon the earth, and sendeth waters upon the fields: To set upon high those that be low; that those which mourn may be exalted to safety.* (Job 5: 8-11).

৵৹৵৹৵৹৵৹

Some Fridays, after hours of clock-watching, Mommy would get the sharp black-handled butcher knife and stand by the door when she heard the elevator door slam and Daddy's keys in the lock. In his hand would be an unfinished can of Budweiser; in his arm he carried a big brown paper bag with a case of the same, a bottle of Colt 45 and a carton of cigarettes—his weekend supply.

"Where were you? Where's the money?" Mommy vehemently inquired.

"I have it—it's in my pocket," Daddy replied staggering and trembling like the lion in the *Wizard of Oz* before he got courage. "Don't point that knife at me."

"Lay the money on the table," Mommy demanded.

Daddy reached into his pants pocket and pulled out a crumbled wad.

"All of it," Mommy austerely said.

Before he sat down, Daddy dug in his shirt pocket and in the front and back of his pants pockets ridding them of all contents and leaving the flaps hanging out as proof. Dwayne and I ran for the coins that fell to the floor and rolled under the table—but we didn't keep them unless Daddy said we could. We could always count on going to bed with some change, thinking we were rich, after Daddy had a few drinks. We'd go to bed happy, yelling to each other from our bedrooms, "What are you going to buy with your money?"

If Mommy wasn't satisfied with the amount of money Daddy placed on the table, it was cause for a fight. But Daddy didn't always accede; he felt he was entitled to spend some of his hard-earned income however he wanted after he had worked two jobs driving a truck and cleaning up offices all week.

Sometimes my sisters and brothers refused to get out of bed for the inevitable. But I couldn't just lie there and try to go to sleep. I stood in the hallway scratching like a mad monkey once, gazing at them in disbelief. Daddy was atop Mommy on the couch choking her. On the brink of an asthma attack, I stood there wheezing and gasping for breath. "Stop Daddy!" I cried through each short breath, tears streaming down my cheeks.

> *Fear came upon me, and trembling, which made all my bones to shake. (Job 4:14).*

"Stop Daddy! Get up! Leave Mommy alone! Don't hurt Mommy. Stop fighting, Daddy!" He'd get up and tell me he wasn't going to hurt her. I believed him.

Daddy sat me on his lap, hugged and kissed me on the cheek, attempting to obliterate from my mind what had just taken place. He would say, "I love you. Do you love me?"

"Yes Daddy, I love you," I responded.

I vowed never to smoke or drink.

CHAPTER IV

UNWANTED

I loved my mother. I loved everybody in the whole world—even the people who picked on me. But I didn't feel my mother truly loved me. She didn't convey it to me like Daddy did. She wasn't the expressive, affectionate type. And her deep tenor voice always sounded so abrasive—like she was constantly fussing.

When my sisters, brothers and me went outside with Mommy, and a neighbor stopped to chat with her, the neighbor would look at us and comment on how we'd all grown. The neighbor would often say of me, "She looks just like her father." Well, that was fine by me because Daddy was a good-looking man. But when Mommy said, "You're just like your father," it didn't have the same connotation. It wasn't meant to be a compliment. And the more she said it as the years went by the more I felt she didn't love me—because she and Daddy didn't get along.

> *Thou shalt be hid from the scourge of the tongue: neither shalt thou be afraid of*

15

*destruction when it cometh. (Job
5:21).*

৯৯৯৯৯৯৯৯

When Daddy was drunk, his alcohol really
talked. He told me that Mommy didn't love me
that much because she didn't want me. He said,
"She wanted Wilhelmina to be the baby girl. She
did everything she could to get rid of you—that's
why you have that rash." He kissed me on my
forehead and assured me that he wanted me and
that he was glad I was born. I loved Daddy more
for sharing that secret with me and for helping me
to understand why Mommy didn't seem to treat
me as well as Wilhelmina.

*Why died I not from the womb?
Why did I not give up the ghost
when I came out of the belly? (Job
3:11).*

৯৯৯৯৯৯৯৯

I hated when Wilhelmina grew out of
something and I got her hand-me-downs because,
when she got something new, she'd rub it in my
face and taunt me about having to wear her old
clothes. With the most evil expression she could

make, Wilhelmina held up or pointed to her new outfits and asserted forcefully to me, "I'd better not catch you in them either!"

Wilhelmina could do no wrong in Mommy's eyes. And, whenever Wilhelmina blamed me for something I got in trouble—when I was innocent. I was distraught that Mommy gave little credence to anything I had to say when it came to Wilhelmina. Her word was pure Gospel and mine—insignificant.

> *Remember, I pray thee, who ever perished, being innocent? Or where were the righteous cut off? Even as I have seen, they that plow iniquity, and sow wickedness, reap the same.* (Job 4:7-8).

CHAPTER V

BLOOD SISTERS AND SUNDAYS

Whenever my elementary school class went on a field trip Daddy made sure I had my fare paid, permission slip signed, a big brown paper bag lunch, and extra money to spend on souvenirs. I was living right up there with the angels—thanks to Daddy. Although it was always at the ninth hour, I could always count on Daddy to come through for me.

Buying lunch and not having to eat in the cafeteria at school was one of the best reasons to go on a class trip. I crossed the street to go up the hill to the delicatessen to buy a spiced ham sandwich with American cheese on Italian hero bread with plenty of spicy deli mustard, lettuce and tomato. And I'd get a kosher-dill pickle from the jar—picking out the biggest one I could find. I would also buy a bag of plain Wise potato chips and a canned soda, which I would place in the freezer overnight. Sometimes I would also get a Ring Ding for dessert. Often, I would double my bag to make certain I wouldn't lose anything. Oh the joy!

Lifted!

By lunchtime, while on our class trip, my bag was often soggy from the pickle, which they wrapped in waxed paper, and the canned soda that defrosted. But I held onto that bag like it was going to fly away if I didn't hold it close.

When the free lunch at school smelled too gross to even look at, particularly the chicken chow mein, my close friend Kay and I would pool our resources. Together, we'd buy a bologna or salami sandwich from the deli on a Kaiser roll or Italian hero bread, and have them cut it and put mustard on my half and mayonnaise on hers. And we'd say, "Would you wrap them separately with two sliced pickles please?" Reluctantly they granted our request.

When others picked on me, Kay stuck by me and sometimes told them off. She lived in my building on the fourth floor. Seldom we'd visit each other at home—most of the time it was at school or in the yard in front of our building. It seemed my mother didn't want me going to my friends' homes too often because she was afraid I'd tell what was going on in ours. "What goes on in this house stays in this house," she often recited. What was the big secret? If everything were fine and fair she wouldn't have to worry about me telling our business. I always kept Kay up on what was going on with me. How could I not—she helped me to cope.

Kay and I became best friends. We each pricked our index finger, rubbed them together and vowed to be "blood sisters." We talked about growing older, being in each other's weddings and making each other our children's godparents. I trusted Kay. She seemed to always know how I felt without me ever having to utter a word. Besides, she and my Daddy share the same birthday, which made her unequivocally special to me.

> *To him that is afflicted pity*
> *should be showed from his friend.*
> *(Job 6:14a).*

ৡৡৡৡৡৡৡ

On Sunday mornings our family arose to the arresting smell of bacon, smoked sausage or salty pork cooking in the skillet; and homemade biscuits or toast in the oven. To accompany the meat, we would have oatmeal, hominy grits, pancakes or eggs. Occasionally, it would be fried chicken wings, white Carolina rice, and from scratch, thick, medium-brown gravy. Tropicana orange juice, Ovaltine or water flushed down the delectable hot breakfast.

The radio would be blasting a sermon or gospel music while Daddy was in the kitchen cooking breakfast; which he sometimes did for an excuse to miss church because then he wouldn't have time to get ready. Sunday was all in the air.

Mommy usually got the bathroom first; then the rest of us would brush our teeth and wash up. We had taken our baths the night before—arguing about who should go first and who didn't wash out their rings. This was our routine always on Saturday nights.

> *How forcible are right words!*
> *But what doth your arguing*
> *reprove? (Job 6:25).*

"Ya'll come on and eat while the food is hot," Daddy yelled from the kitchen as we dressed in our Sunday best. Wilhelmina and I usually had about two good dresses that we rotated wearing every other Sunday. And we wore black patent leather shoes that we cleaned and shined with Vaseline. I was pretty proud of how well I shined my shoes to make them look new when it was past time for a new pair.

No one could touch the plates, as we savored the appetizing aroma from the edibles spread before us until we were all seated and said grace. I loved Sunday mornings at the breakfast table. Family time. One person was always designated to read "The Lord's Prayer" or "The Twenty-Third Psalm," while the rest of us repeated each verse in unison. I usually volunteered because I knew it by heart. Occasionally Daddy went with us to church; other times he'd stay home and prepare dinner or sleep.

Later on, after the sun set a little, Daddy would go downstairs to spend time with his drinking buddies in the parking lot. Mommy hated him drinking, particularly in public—especially on Sundays. Daddy and his buddies weren't blatant with their bottles—just their cans (which they wrapped in brown paper bags to disguise the contents). They tried to make it appear as though they were drinking soda. Kay's father was one of his partners. A group of them would hide each other or they would get into one of their cars to turn their bottles up. Although intoxicated, when Daddy came back upstairs, he usually had Neapolitan ice cream and a pound cake for dessert, or a huge, sweet oval watermelon.

Many Sunday nights were spent with the family gathered around our black and white television.

Lifted!

We watched *Lassie*, *The Ed Sullivan Show* or *Walt Disney*. When *Walt Disney* was going to be exceptionally good, we were permitted to go next door to our white neighbors house to watch it in color. Few white people lived in our building, which consisted of twenty-one floors with eleven apartments on each floor. Our neighbors, an elderly couple, were the only whites on our floor. They always invited us to come over and we'd sit on their carpeted floor pretending we were at the Loew's Theatre.

CHAPTER VI

TEACHER'S PET

My attire was long-sleeved dresses, turtlenecks, blouses with a collar and opaque tights—even in one hundred degree temperatures. I constantly tugged at my sleeves and collar to make sure my skin was sufficiently hidden, and I would hold my sleeves in my hands while writing in school.

My sixth grade classmates called me "ugly" so much that I was convinced I was. When I got out of the bathtub and looked in the mirror at myself I often cried because my skin was odious and grave looking. Who could love me?

> *They that hate thee shall be clothed with shame; and the dwelling place of the wicked shall come to nought.* (Job 8:22).

ళ్ళ్ళ్ళ్ళ్ళ్ళ్

As much as I abhorred fights and altercations, my penchant for scratching benefited me once when my classmates instigated a fight between a boy and me. When our class was dismissed from school for the day some of my classmates nudged a guy hard up against my back. I turned around, threw my books to the ground in front of the school, and started attacking. My head was bent down and tucked in the whole time to protect my face, my arms rowed like a cat clawing a cork wall. I didn't want to fight, but I was tired of being treated like a despicable object. I had no recourse but to defend myself.

A crowd of kids said I won the fight as they gathered up my books and escorted me home like I was queen for a day; but I didn't feel like a victor. I had no idea and was not concerned about who had won. I was wondering what was going to happen tomorrow.

While standing in line on the school grounds the next morning, a woman I had never seen before came over to me pointing her index finger and shaking it in my face. It was his mother. She began threatening me, saying, "Don't you ever put your hands on my son again! If you do you have me to answer to. Do you hear me?"

> *If I be wicked, why then labor I in vain?* (Job 9:29).

Although motionless, tears fell freely while I listened to that big woman harass me for beating up her son. He was bigger than me; I didn't initiate the fight. Did she really know how the fight started? Didn't she care? Why isn't my mother here defending me? I cried all day. After a while, my teacher let me stand out in the hallway until I regained my composure.

It wasn't until the next day that I actually noticed that I had nearly scratched the living daylights out of my classmate. His face was all bruised, swollen and punctured. I could hardly believe my eyes. Did I do that? Well, maybe they will leave me alone now, I thought.

> **Let him take his rod away from**
> **me, and let not his fear terrify me.**
> *(Job 9:34).*

৯৯৯৯৯৯৯৯

Ms. Herringson was my favorite teacher in the whole world. She was in her mid-twenties, of average height, with a pallid ivory complexion and cinnamon shoulder-length hair. Her mother came to visit our class a couple of times to watch her teach because it was her first teaching job out of college. I automatically admired her mother.

Ms. Herringson called me "Nettie." No one had ever called me Nettie before. It was endearing to me and made me feel special. She would always compliment me and tell me I was doing a good job. She said that I had good penmanship and that I wrote well. Ever since then I wanted to write.

Whenever Ms. Herringson asked, "Who would like to stay after and clean the blackboard?" Quickly, my hand flew into the air. I hoped she would choose me. When I was selected to erase and wash the blackboard I did it slowly because I wanted to prolong my time with Ms. Herringson. Sometimes she let me assist her in grading the class papers. It felt good to hang around someone who seemed genuinely to care about me.

Once or twice during the school year Ms. Herringson called out my full name instead of saying Nettie. Whenever she did this, it was a cue to the entire class that she was not in a good mood that day. Some of my classmates called me "Teacher's Pet," thinking they were upsetting me; but I liked it. When I graduated from her class into Junior High School she still spent time with me during the summer, invited me to her house to make brownies, took me to museums, to Lincoln Center for the Performing Arts, and to lunch.

Oftentimes I'd go back to the school to visit her and inform her of my grades so that she would be proud of me. She got married, had a son, and we lost contact. But I'll never forget Ms. Herringson. Never.

> *Thou hast granted me life and favor, and thy visitation hath preserved my spirit.* *(Job 10:12).*

CHAPTER VII

MOMMA

My family often spent our summers in North Carolina because both our parents are from there. Daddy drove us 500 miles down south in his Buick, but he couldn't stay because he had to go back to work. After a month or so he came back to get us. His mother (Grandma) lived in the country and owned a huge farm with every animal you can name, fruit trees and patches with all kinds of vegetables. Grandma was eager to have us spend time at her house and give us crates of peaches, tomatoes and okra. "Yeech, okra!" It smelled nauseating cooking and looked like olive snot—but the adults savored the taste.

My brothers, sisters and I took turns swinging on the tire that hung from the tree and on the swing with a wooden seat that fell off while you were in mid-air and left your rear-end sore. We trampled in bare feet in the cool, sparkling clear creeks, ran through bobbed-wire pigpens and chased chickens. Actually, we ran from the chickens!

When we needed to excrete we had to use the outhouse or "slop jar"—a white enameled pail beside our bed that had a red line around the rim, with a lid. At nighttime we preferred using the slop jar, because we refused to walk ten yards to the outhouse in the still darkness. Besides, all kinds of sounds could be heard that we weren't terribly accustomed to.

Most of our cousins, aunts and uncles on my mother's side lived in town. We took turns staying in the country and in town. We preferred staying in town because we could use an indoor toilet that flushed; we had more relatives our age there; and there were stores at our disposal.

In our bare feet, we strolled down the dirt roads with our cousins to the Dairy Queen and corner candy store. As we passed the neighbors houses they waved from their porches saying, "Aren't you the Covington children from New York?"

Astonished, we replied, "Yes Ma'am. Yes Sir."

While down south, during the summer of 1970 (I was twelve), we learned that our grandmother, Momma (who lived closed to town), was given a short time to live. She had ovarian cancer. It was detected too late because she would never go to see a doctor.

Momma lived in New York City, on the second floor of a tenement apartment, with a fire escape, across the street from us, until she moved back home to North Carolina. Often, I spent my weekends with Momma. I enjoyed accompanying her to the quaint, storefront church she attended. She was a preacher; my mother's mother.

At Momma's church in Harlem, some of the members played the accordion, electric guitar, harmonica, tambourine, and the washboard. The soulfully gratifying sound of all the musical instruments resonated onto the avenue and sometimes drew a crowd. People came in off the street just to enjoy the reverberation. It was a fine way to draw in souls.

I learned to beat the tambourine and washboard well, which I found to be a real art; and occasionally I was asked to sing a solo. "*I m pressing on, I m pressing on,*" I'd sing with all seriousness of mind, heart and spirit with my eyes tightly shut and my head up in the air. I felt God's presence.

At Momma's church some people were at the altar praying aloud, others rolled on the floor. Strange sounds protruded from their mouths that I did not understand. The missionary mothers sprang over and quickly draped a cloth or sweater around the rolling women's legs to help keep them chaste, and the brothers safe.

Some of the members carried on rejoicing like God was right there in that building and they were going to be caught up right then and there with Him. I wondered how in the world could some of the big women jump so high, move so swiftly and dance so gracefully.

When my sisters and brothers came to the church with my mother they laughed and ridiculed the strange babble. But I didn't. I was too afraid to "play with God." They would go home and mimic the people until they had each other rolling on the floor dripping with laughter.

> *My lips shall not speak wickedness, nor my tongue utter deceit.* *(Job 27:4).*

Sometimes after morning worship I had the privilege of dining at a restaurant with Momma and some of the elderly sisters. Other times we went back to her apartment to eat before returning for evening service. Momma would fix us both a cup of hot tea with milk in it. I had to acquire a taste for it because I was only used to drinking tea plain, or with lemon. After acquiring a taste for tea with milk, I'd think of Momma whenever I would drink a cup.

Almost every time I spent the night with Momma, I'd see a mouse. They often appeared in the eyes of the gas stove and would have a field day running around playfully and eating the spilled food particles. I was terrified of mice (we didn't have them in the projects), but I relished the time spent with Momma more than I feared the mice, so I kept going back. Because I was afraid to kneel on the floor to say my prayers, I got on my knees in the bed. I usually quoted "The Lord's Prayer" and "Psalms 23" twice before I got to the God blesses. Then I'd roll over and fall asleep forgetting all about the squeaking rodents that would have a hay day during the night.

> **Thou shalt make thy prayer unto Him, and He shall hear thee, and thou shalt pay thy vows.** *(Job 22:27)*.

ৡৡৡৡৡৡৡ

In August 1970, in North Carolina, Momma lay in the bed dying. We both loved Nabisco butter cookies, so I bought a box and shared them with her. The next day, one of my aunts rolled

Momma over to wash her and found cookie crumbs and a mass of ants on the sheets. I felt awful for Momma. I was only gently scolded because everyone knew how well Momma and I loved each other and that she wouldn't want them to fuss at me. I was safe.

I didn't want to lose Momma; but God wanted her. He didn't want her to suffer any longer. It was her time to leave this old earthly tabernacle behind.

I had no prior recollection of ever attending a funeral. Momma's was the first. The sun shone brilliantly and there were no clouds in the sky. Mommy bought me a beautiful navy v-necked dress with a white lace collar. My skin was exposed, except my legs. But it was okay.

On the way to the church, Momma's corpse was escorted by the police and followed by a huge entourage of cars. The line of cars extended so far, that even on our knees looking out the rear window from a hill, there appeared to be no end to the line. Each driver had on his headlights and the traffic was halted at every intersection. Momma was a noble woman who knew a lot of people and she was loved royally.

I scratched myself into a furious frenzy at Momma's funeral and during the interment. I lacerated the backs of my legs so dreadfully that blood and pus oozed through my white opaque hose. When I beheld my legs, gnats and flies had swarmed to the sores and were feasting. I swatted them and killed them where they lay. I was utterly grief-stricken and could hardly walk because of the pain and stiffness from the open wounds. I yearned to be back at the house to rip off my clothes.

> *My flesh is clothed with worms and clods of dust; my skin is broken, and become loathsome. . .And though after my skin worms destroy this body, yet in my flesh shall I see God.* (Job 7:5; 19:26).

CHAPTER VIII

RASHY-ASHY

In Junior High School, I wore opaque tights faithfully so no one could see my legs through them. But sometimes when I'd come home from school they would have blood and a yellow, sticky, liquid substance on them where I had been scratching. The hose would cleave to my skin when I tried to take them off and it would hurt causing me horrendous discomfort. But not only did my hose adhere to my skin, so did my other garments where my skin was terribly ruptured. I had to peel off my bra and panties because the pus that had seeped out and dried had glued my clothing to my skin.

> *By the great force of my disease is my garment changed. . . I cry unto thee, and thou dost not hear me: I stand up, and thou regardest me not. (Job 30:18a, 20).*

I feared my nipples wouldn't grow back because every time I undressed I was peeling off layers of skin as if I was removing adhesive tape.

Lifted!

The odor contained in my skin and clothing, produced by the open wounds combined with the ointment, was completely repulsive. The lining in the cups of my bras would still have scales in them after they had been laundered.

> *Doth not He see my ways, and count all my steps?* (Job 31:4).

I scratched my eyebrows out and they wouldn't grow back because my skin was too irritated and cracked. To place my hands in water or to bathe was extremely painful—soap would sting immensely. Water burned my skin like alcohol drowning on an open sore.

Some of my classmates picked on me, threw erasers at me and followed me home calling me cruel names like "Rashy-ashy." The girls made fun of me by pretending to scratch behind their legs, forearms, or neck the way I did. Then they would giggle hysterically until they almost fell off their seats. In Hygiene, while we were learning about venereal diseases, the students passed an object around in class like a hot potato and said it had the "V.C. germ," using my initials.

> *My friends scorn me: but mine eye poureth out tears unto God. .*

Vanessa G. Cunningham

*.How long will ye vex my soul,
and break me in pieces with
words?* (Job 16:20; 19:2).

৵৽৵৽৵৽৵৽

Once, in an elevator filled with people, after an uncivilized day at school, a young girl embarrassed me when she asked, "Were you burned in a fire?"

"No," I responded calmly.

"How come you don't have any eyebrows?" she persisted.

The fifteenth floor, finally. I exited the elevator without answering or looking back.

I did all I could to try to get my mother and siblings to love me. When it was their turn to take the clothes to the Laundromat or wash dishes, I would sometimes wash them instead so they would like me. Mommy said I always did a good job. I wanted to please her, so I did my best. I volunteered to go to the store and run errands. Whatever it took to make my family want me, love me, I would acquiesce.

৵৽৵৽৵৽৵৽

I was thirteen when I won a scholarship through my Junior High School to attend a nature camp for four weeks during the summer of 1971. It was going to be my first experience away from home for that length of time and I was skeptical about leaving. I wasn't keen on rustic living so I was reluctant to leave the shelter of our three-bedroom insulated apartment. My close friend, Kay, had also won a scholarship and agreed to go only if I did. We resolved that if we had each other we would feel less detached, so we went as partners.

That summer my eczema flared up so terribly that it seemed at its peak. The doctors thought it might do me some good to be outdoors in the fresh, open air; so Mommy and Daddy made sure I had the provisions I needed to go away. They bought me a trunk, raincoat, flashlight, and a host of other necessities that were listed.

When the time came, Mommy took me downtown to the Port Authority Bus Terminal where we were supposed to meet all the other campers to depart on two buses. All the parents said their good-byes, and we were on our way. I felt I was being discarded.

Our all-girls camp consisted of campers of all nationalities from various countries, including Poland. On weekends we had chaperoned visits from the neighboring all-boys camp. Kay was the athletic type and fairly outdoorsy for a city girl.

We shared the same cabin with two other girls. Many of the guys were attracted to her for her outer beauty and figure, but she didn't abandon me.

When "care packages" came most of the girls would share their bundle of goodies. The camaraderie was awesome and no one knew to call me "Rashy-ashy." Each morning we were awakened at 6:00 a.m. sharp and had to hurry into the shower. We did exercises before breakfast as if we were in boot camp and followed in rows to eat breakfast in our mess hall.

Our schedule was planned for us and we were highly encouraged to participate in the activities. We hiked in the woods for miles, planted, and had recreational time to either play outdoor sports or indoor table games. I usually chose to remain indoors to play pinochle because I hated when bugs would feast on the mucilaginous exudates from my broken, sweaty skin.

The campers were compelled to learn to swim. I hated swimming because I abhorred putting on a swimsuit for everyone to see my body—my skin. I didn't want to be in the water with everyone else because I felt dirty beside their bright white skin. If my own sister hated sitting next to me and getting in water with me why did I want to subject strangers to sharing the same water? Rather than

have them despise me, I withdrew from them. I
told the counselors I was too afraid I'd have an
asthma attack holding my breath under the water
so they didn't make me get in. But I still had to
wear a bathing suit. I was so grateful it was not a
coed camp.

After three weeks at camp everyone was excited
about "family day." We had mailed invitations
inviting our family members to visit us. It was
about a two-to-three-hour trip for my family so I
wasn't sure who would come—if anyone. My
two sisters came. I was both relieved and
pleasantly surprised.

Everyone thought Wilhelmina was my mother
because she was tall for her age—fourteen; and
that day she looked particularly grown-up in her
forest green and white dress and white shoes.
Most everyone else's mother came—including
Kay's.

CHAPTER IX

NOW I LAY ME DOWN TO SLEEP

In my early teens I ingested over 47 pills of various sorts—whatever was in the medicine cabinet—after writing a letter to my family and leaving it in my Bible. I tried to end my life because I didn't think life was worth living feeling unloved.

> *What is my strength, that I should hope? And what is mine end, that I should prolong my life? My face is foul with weeping, and on my eyelids is the shadow of death. Even that it would please God to destroy me; that He would let loose His hand, and cut me off! (Job 6:11; 16:16; 6:9).*

But God said, "No!" It was not my time to die. I lay down to pass away, but He would not let me go. I found my way to the bathroom and began regurgitating uncontrollably into the toilet. Most of the pills appeared to have been vomited up. I wasn't really sure and I didn't really care.

Lifted!

My mother heard me throwing up, saw the blackness in the toilet, and yelled at me. Somehow she knew what I had done without my ever having revealed a word. My stomach ached, I felt so sick. She gave me a hot cup to drink while I was still standing over the toilet. "What is it?" I asked.

"Drink it," she said angrily. "It's coffee with mineral oil in it. It will make you throw up."

I sipped it and was purged. I guess I'd nearly poisoned myself to death by mixing all the different medications because all of the fluid came up black. It mattered not to me. My tongue was dark purple and black for weeks and my breath was absolutely foul. I was not taken to the hospital to have my stomach pumped or anything. I guess that was a way of keeping things quiet.

After the purging, Mommy made me drink black coffee to keep me awake. She sat me on her bed and said, "What will my friends think if you kill yourself?"

> *Wherefore is light given to him that is in misery, and life unto the bitter in soul; Which long for death, but it cometh not; and dig for it more than for hid treasures; Which rejoice exceedingly, and*

are glad, when they can find the grave? (Job 3:20-22).

&~&~&~&~&~&~&~

My eldest sister, Gayle, was planning her wedding for Saturday, August 20, 1972. For me it was D-day—my first true introduction to abandonment. I was happy for Gayle, but terrified for myself. She took up for me when others bothered me. Sometimes when we played Scrabble, Monopoly or Pokeno at home or over friend's homes I would get teased about my skin and Gayle would make everyone leave me alone. When we'd go ice-skating with our friends in Central Park, Gayle would shadow me. She took me under her breast and guarded me as a tiger protects its newborn felines. With Gayle around me I felt safe.

Who would be around to shelter me now when Daddy was at work? Who would efface the hurt I felt when Mommy poured cold water on my face from her drinking glass while I lay playing on the kitchen floor—just because she wanted to. Who would provide a sealant for my inner and outer wounds?

Lifted!

৯৹৹৹৹৹৹৹

Wilhelmina and I were part of the bridal party. We wore aqua-colored gowns with long gloves to our elbows. I believe Gayle considered me when she had the seamstress design our attire. Our fingers were exposed, but the gloves did the concealing job I needed. Gayle also permitted me to have my gloves sewn to the sleeve of my dress so that they would not slide down my arms.

When the photos came back I didn't want Gayle to show them because I looked like a vaudevillian with a black mask. I looked like a spook. Who could love me; for what reason?

CHAPTER X

TAKE ME TO THE WATER

One Sunday night in January 1973, my friend, David, took me on my first date to the Pentecostal church he attended. We used to attend Sunday school together and sing in the choir at the Baptist Church our parents brought us up in. Now he was "born again" and was "called" into the ministry. Excited just wouldn't suffice to describe how I anticipated going on this date—even though we were just going to church. My outfit had to be just right— long sleeves, a turtleneck and opaque stockings. I didn't want to embarrass him by letting anybody see any of my skin that I could hide. Gayle was excited for me and wanted to make sure I looked nice so she brought over one of her dresses for me to wear. It was a straight burgundy and white polyester dress with a twelve-inch zipper down the front, long sleeves and a collar.

I was in the tenth grade and had just turned fifteen a month prior, David was sixteen in the eleventh. I guess he discerned I was lonely and searching for love and happiness when we ran into each other in the school park near our buildings.

That's when he invited me to church. To him it might not have really been an official "date"—but it was to me.

The church was walking distance from the projects where we lived—just about five blocks. Although it was winter, I was warm; I felt like a queen striding down the street with him by my side. The feeling was too good to be true, unforgettable. I wanted to seize and savor every moment and not mess things up by saying the wrong thing, so I said nothing.

We entered the sanctuary at about 7:30 p.m. It was all bedecked with royal blue carpet and pew seats to match. The multicolored jewel-toned stained glass window above the baptismal pool reflected the light like a kaleidoscope. There were a lot of young people singing in the Radio Broadcast Choir, including David. I didn't have the pleasure of sitting next to him in church, which was a little disappointing; but it was probably best anyway. Church was for worshipping God.

David introduced me to some of his friends and had me to sit with them. All over the temple people in the congregation on the main floor and the balcony were worshipping, clapping their hands in unison and singing praises unto God with piano, organ and drums accompaniment. The atmosphere was ethereal! It reminded me of the times I went to church with Momma—only there were many more people here.

The broadcast lasted one hour, but service continued. Some people gave testimonies about the blessings that God had wrought in their lives. And during the sermon, all over the building people were jumping up and shouting, "Preach Bishop! Amen! Hallelujah! Thank you Lord! That's the word!" It was like a big party. Everyone was happy and in a celebratory spirit.

When service was over, as unattractive as I was with this hideous-looking rash covering 100% of my neck and 98% of my face, the members hugged and kissed me when they greeted me. I was baffled at the display of love expressed to me by strangers. They reached out to me and embraced me as ugly as I was. The fellowship was unlike anything I had ever known.

I frequented the services after that and was baptized in "Jesus' name." I had already been baptized before, but during altar call some of David's friends, who I always sat with while he was in the choir, kept reciting, "You need The Name. You need The Name." They said, "Father, Son and Holy Ghost are just titles. You have a father, and he has a name. Father is his title. Your father has a son, and son is his title, but not his name. The Holy Ghost is the title for the Spirit of God."

"Do you see what we're saying?" one sister asked as I stared at her.

"In the Bible," a brother continued, "Jesus says, I and my father are one. That means Jesus the son, and God the father, are one. They are the same. There aren't three separate life forms. God the father, God the son, and God the Holy Ghost are three in one. The scripture says we should be baptized in the name of Jesus for remission of sins and you shall receive the gift of the Holy Ghost; but it's not in the titles. The titles can't save you. It's the blood that Jesus shed on Calvary that makes the difference."

All I could think of was that whatever it was they had, I wanted it; and whatever it took to get it was worth it. What did I have to lose by getting baptized again? If being submerged in the name of Jesus was all I needed to do to experience that joy, I wanted to do it.

I walked down the left center aisle toward the altar and said, "I want to be baptized in Jesus' name." I was the only soul going down for baptism that night in that huge church, but I didn't care. It seemed everyone else in there had already been to the water and they weren't paying much attention to me because they were caught up "in the Spirit."

> *Canst thou by searching find out God? Canst thou find out the Almighty unto perfection? If thou prepare thine heart, and stretch out thine hands toward Him; If iniquity be in thine hand, put it far away, and let not wickedness dwell in thy tabernacles. For then shalt thou lift thy face without spot; yea, thou shalt be steadfast, and shalt not fear. (Job 11:7, 13-15).*

CHAPTER XI

SAVED

One of the ministers on the pulpit gestured to the missionaries in maxi and tea-length black dresses with white collars and felt black hats, who were all sitting together in a group in a designated area down front, to take me in the back to get me ready for baptism. The women gave me instructions to completely undress and put on some prepared white garments, swimming cap and socks. The congregation was singing: "*Take me to the water to be baptized.*"

"God is going to wash away all of yours sins and you are going to rise to walk in the newness of life," said one of the stout women resolutely. Then they led me to the pool.

The minister in the pool reached out his hand to me as I walked down four steps into the clear, still water. The water was frigid—not much different from the temperature outside, but it mattered not to me. As he placed my hands to my chest he took his left hand and placed it atop mine. He then placed his right behind me to guard my back. The minister bowed his head and began to pray aloud fervently. Silence abruptly permeated the church. All was hushed; the minister and I appeared to be alone in the sanctuary.

"Lord," he said, and continued:

> *We thank you for this beloved daughter who has come confessing her sins and her belief in the death, burial and resurrection of Jesus Christ.*
>
> *Lord, we are asking you, right now, to let your blood prevail. Wash her thoroughly from her sins and cleanse her from her iniquities, in the name of Our Lord and Savior Jesus Christ— and she shall receive the gift of the Holy Ghost. In Jesus' name. Amen.*

The minister then completely immersed my body into the chilling water and I arose to roaring thunder. The musicians began playing a vivacious tune while the energized congregation sang and danced over the one soul who submitted her life to Christ.

Afterwards, some of the missionaries who had helped to prepare me for baptism said, "Lift up your hands Sister Vonnette, and say Hallelujah!"

"Hallelujah," I responded, as they walked me downstairs to a dimly lit prayer room that resembled a huge walk-in closet to receive the Holy Ghost speaking in tongues.

The carpet was scarlet with benches all around the walls for kneeling. A powerful, spiritual aura manifested the area. I knelt down and two sisters knelt beside me, one sister on my right and the other on my left. They told me to think about how Jesus was nailed to the cross; how he shed his blood that we would have a right to the tree of life; how they pierced Him in His sides and put a crown of thorns on His head; how He died and rose again; and how His blood washed away my sins.

"Give thanks to God and ask Him to fill you and anoint you with His spirit. Let Jesus in. Let Him control your speech," they said concurrently. And they persisted:

> *Think about how good God has been to you. He loves you when no one else loves you.*
>
> *Now, lift your hands and thank the Lord for what He has done. Say thank you Jesus! Say Hallelujah! Praise Him! Praise Him! Yes! That's it! Praise Him!*

*That's it! Come on. Let Him have
His way! That's it! That's it!*

I said thank you Jesus and Hallelujah with tears
streaming until I felt God's presence all through
me from the crown of my head unto the soles of
my feet. I began speaking in an unknown
language. I didn't know what I was saying, but I
knew I was communing directly with God, and He
understood me. There was "a oneness." I felt
complete and renewed. I had received the Holy
Ghost speaking in tongues as the Spirit of God
gave me the utterance. I was saved!

I joined that congregation, which became my
refuge and the source of my strength—my reason
for living. Often, my family ostracized me for
going to church too much. Who could not love it?

The women were taught that a woman's hair is
her glory and it should be covered with a hat or
something before entering church as reverence to
the Holy Spirit. The members said it was written
in the Bible in the New Testament. I read the
scripture and followed suit. I didn't want to be
disobedient or out of order.

Most of the time the women wore lace cloths
secured by a bobby pin or two that looked like
doilies. They came in multiple colors to match
any outfit and were called "prayer caps." I was so

saved I wore them in the street when I left church and felt no shame. I even wore them on the bus and the subway. I was not ashamed. I was proud of the Jesus in me.

Occasionally, when one of the sisters didn't have a prayer cap or hat on, one of the missionaries or other sisters would pull a tissue out of their pocketbook, provide two bobby pins, and insist that they put it on their head. Generally, you could tell the visitors and the oblivious by the napkins or tissues upon their heads.

My church family and I became blood-related through the shedding of Christ's blood on the cross. He made us one. They didn't pick on me or reject me, and no one acted as if they were better than I. We had all things in common.

Some Sundays when church was over I would bring one of the sister's home with me as long as it was okay with my parents. They would either bring their own food or have dinner with us when there was enough. On the way home we'd pass the parking lot where my Daddy hang out. I'd look over to see if he was there—which he usually was if he wasn't already upstairs. I'd introduce him to my friend and he'd say to his buddies (who already knew who I was), "That's my daughter," pointing to me. "She goes to that big holiness church." I'd walk away beaming.

Wilhelmina and Dwayne said we were all crazy— "Holy rollers." They didn't seem to understand my relationship with my new brothers and sisters in Christ, and they would complain about me embarrassing them because I walked home and into our building "with that thing on my head." I wasn't much understood before I joined the church nor after.

> *I am as one mocked of his neighbor, who calleth upon God, and He answereth him: the just upright man is laughed to scorn. Oh that ye would altogether hold your peace! And it should be your wisdom. (Job 12:4; 13:5).*

CHAPTER XII

IN-LOVE

I had fallen in love with David. He called it an infatuation, but I knew better. I had never known what it was like to feel the way I did until David. My stomach fluttered and I stumbled over words when we were together because I was always trying to be perfect. I was willing to do almost anything and go anywhere as long as I could have him in my life.

I wasn't obsessed with him, but I yearned for his love. When he walked me home and to my door I was never "forward"—always a lady. As long as he didn't initiate an embrace I wasn't going to.

After several months, he finally kissed me on the cheek! I was ready to meet my Maker. God had just been too good to let this come to pass for me. I couldn't ask Him for another thing!

As time passed, David invited me to go to Rye Play Land, Great Adventure, and Coney Island with his family. Heaven on earth! "Lord, hold back the moon." I didn't want the days to end.

David and I were enrolled in an Upward Bound program at Columbia University the summer of

Vanessa G. Cunningham

1974. Columbia was walking distance from my home and David would occasionally walk me home. He stayed on campus, but I commuted. We were in a creative writing class together and it was sheer glory! Besides God—he was my reason for living.

In a couple of weeks David would be leaving to go away to college and I was going to miss him sorely. I wanted him to say, "Vonnette, I love you. Will you wait for me?" I wanted him to say he wanted me to be his forever before he left.

A full moon illuminated the sky brilliantly one evening while we sat on a bench on campus talking. The heavens pronounced the eminence of God and radiated in my soul. Could I be more euphoric?

The next evening I wrote this poem:

"First Love"

I loved him
And thought I could never love anyone else
I did not want to
Christ was my first love
But he came second

When I was down
Just seeing him made me elated
He didn't even have to speak
Just his presence made me contented

Lifted!

I loved him so much
'Til I was afraid to love
Not wanting it to ever end
Afraid of what the end might be like

Then
One day we had a talk
We both told each other that we loved one another
That seemed the happiest day of my life
It was as if I was being reborn
As if something dead in me had just taken root and
blossomed

The day after
We had another talk
He told me that he loved me as he loved his parents
He told me that he loved me as a sister

I didn't say anything
I just sat there
Still
Trying not to cry
But how could I not?
It seemed impossible
The tears flowed without an invitation

I didn't only want to be his sister!

I got up
As if something had just exploded out of a socket
I began to walk in strides
Determined not to look back
Not wanting him to see me sob
Why didn't he tell me that yesterday?
When he first told me that he loved me

Instead
He had me thinking I would be the woman in his life

I didn't blame him, but rather myself
For ever getting involved
For ever loving as hard as I did
For giving my heart away

It was the beginning of hell for me
Not realizing heaven still existed
I wanted to kill myself
Not caring about ever going to heaven

But somehow, with God's help
I was able to bring myself together

I wanted to hate him
But I didn't
I couldn't
I still loved him
And even now
He still has a small piece of my heart
Which will always be his

My first love

જીજીજીજીજીજીજી

I knew that some of the others sisters at church liked David as I did, so I didn't let them know what he really meant to me in order to avoid conflict. I was blessed that he cared as much for me as he did—with my bad skin.

CHAPTER XIII

WOUNDED AND DESERTED

Afew days later, one sunlit afternoon when I arrived home from the Upward Bound program, I walked past my parents' bedroom and heard, "She's putting me out, Nette." These were the somber words my father lamented that I don't cease to recall. What was I going to do with my Daddy gone? It was unthinkable, grievous. I did not want my father to leave. I did not want him to leave me. My eldest brother and sister were married and gone but Wilhelmina, Dwayne and I remained.

I was sixteen, entering my senior year in High School, and I had to adjust to not having my father around. He had been my safeguard, my protector. I could always depend on him. How was I going to get along without him?

Whenever we were sick Daddy made up a concoction with Jack Daniel's, honey, and lemon; it burned your chest when you swallowed it, but by morning you were singing his praises. And whenever we went Easter shopping or to the doctor in the Bronx, Daddy always pulled into

White Castle. We didn't have one in Manhattan, so this was always a real treat for the entire family.

And when the holidays rolled around or during the summer months Daddy always drove the family to the mountains for a picnic or to Orchard Beach or the Bronx Zoo. Once in a while we'd go as far as Atlantic City. We could invite friends to come along as long as there was room in the car and we had behaved. Sometimes several carloads followed us when Daddy convinced his friends to drive.

Gayle was gone; David was leaving, and now Daddy.

Just in time, I gave my life to Christ and learned He would be with me always and would never leave me nor forsake me. He would be my deliverer—my solace, my hope.

> *For I know that my redeemer liveth, and that He shall stand at the latter day upon the earth. (Job 19:25).*

Lifted!

My parents were separated and my mother was at choir rehearsal one Tuesday night when Wilhelmina and I got into a dispute because I was drawing her black wool glove. My assignment for Art class was to draw a still-life in pencil, with shading. I placed the glove on the lamp table just below the light and sat on the side of the bed I inherited after Gayle got married.

Wilhelmina wasn't in the room at the time I started, but she came in the back to see what I was doing. When she saw I was drawing her glove, she snatched it up and threw it on her bed. She dared me to touch it, and left the room.

I never challenged Wilhelmina. It wasn't worth it. I never won. But this time I was doing my homework—and it was just a glove. I wasn't wearing it or anything. So I picked it up and proceeded to arrange it the way I had it to complete my drawing. She came back and again, grabbed it, and threw it on her bed. "You'd better leave my glove alone," she threatened, looking mean and evil.

I was nearly finished with my drawing when I heard Wilhelmina coming down the hall into the bedroom for the third time. I wrapped the glove around my left hand and held onto it for dear life. She pulled and tugged on it to try and jerk it away, but I would not let it go. She dragged me into the hallway near my brother's room saying, "You'd better let go. You'd better let go. If you don't let go I'm going to hurt you."

I didn't. I was fed up. I didn't want her to win. It was not fair! I was blameless, and sick and tired of her bullying me.

Wilhelmina dug her nails into my hand to force me to surrender. I wouldn't. Instead, I began to plead the blood aloud saying, "The blood of Jesus! The blood of Jesus!"

She and Dwayne laughed so hard until he was howling on the floor holding his stomach. She was so infuriated with me that a couple of tears rolled down her face. She was not used to me defending myself against her in this manner. She kept demanding, "Let my glove go! Let it go! I'm going to hurt you." But I was determined to hold on until I could stand the pain no longer. I thought about Jesus on the cross being persecuted and pierced when He had not deserved it. On principle, I held on until I could no longer bear the pain. My hand was sore and bleeding slightly but I wasn't sorry that I didn't yield.

I called Gayle to tell her what happened and she tried to mediate—to no avail. When my mother came home she made us apologize—as usual, me first. I looked Wilhelmina in the face and was sincere in my apology—even though I didn't believe I did anything wrong.   But she neither gazed at me, nor did she genuinely apologize—although she did utter something under her breath.

I never liked discord, arguments or confrontations.   I just wanted everybody to get along and love each other.

I never got to finish my drawing.

> *Though He slay me, yet will I trust in Him: but I will maintain mine own ways before Him. He also shall be my salvation: for a hypocrite shall not come before Him. (Job 13:15-16).*

CHAPTER XIV

RED

I was delighted whenever my mother permitted me to go to my girlfriend's house on the seventh floor. I called her "Red" because her hair would turn auburn in the sun. Red called me "Nettie"—the same name my favorite teacher called me. When we were together we held nothing back. We spilled our guts. Red and I became best friends during our early teens, like Kay and I were. Kay and I were still bonded, but she had a boyfriend.

Red and I attended the same High School in the Bronx. We would faithfully meet each other on the porch or in the lobby to walk to the Broadway train station together to catch the Number One Local. While riding the train to school I informed Red of the dispute Wilhelmina and I had. Red knew I hated contention; so did she. I showed her the pills I had brought with me and told her I was contemplating suicide. Unbeknownst to me, when she got to school she called her mother, who called the school, who called my mother.

The principal made an announcement over the loudspeaker for me to come to the main office.

My teacher dismissed me. To say the least, I was bewildered and embarrassed to have my name broadcast over the loudspeaker, as if I were a criminal.

The counselor in the office said, "Give me the drugs you are carrying."

Drugs, I thought. What drugs? I didn't have any drugs; didn't do any drugs, and didn't have much knowledge of drugs. They had me confused.

"The pills—give me the pills," she demanded.

Red! It was nobody but Red. No one else knew I had pills on me. Why did she tell the school? I wasn't angry with her. I guess she just didn't want to lose her best friend.

The counselor informed my mother that I was in need of counseling and she recommended a psychologist in our neighborhood near Columbia. I began attending a nearby therapy group in the lower level of a huge Catholic church with people of similar age. I really didn't understand why I was there; but I learned to adapt because it was an opportunity to get away from home for an hour and be with people who didn't criticize and belittle me.

After a short while, family therapy was recommended but no one else ever attempted to go because I was the only one with a problem. And, it was only my problem.

I am full of confusion; therefore see thou mine affliction; For it increaseth. (Job 10:15b-16a).

৯৯৯৯৯৯৯৯

David and I often corresponded by mail though my heart ached for his presence. With great anticipation I awaited his return home during holidays and school breaks. In David's absence, however, I continued my devotion to God and was faithful to the church. On Friday nights I occasionally stayed to all-night prayer, which lasted from midnight until 6:00 a.m. I was elected to be our youth choir chaplain and chosen as a prayer warrior because of my commitment to prayer. On occasion, I led songs with the choir and traveled out of state with the church to conventions and fellowships.

Often, late at night I would stay up late drinking hot Lipton tea, eating saltine crackers and reading my Bible while everyone else slept. As I delved into the Word and memorized verses that seemed to jump out at me, my knowledge and understanding of the Bible greatly increased.

Lifted!

CHAPTER XV

SPIRITUAL
GUIDANCE AND DIRECTION

One of the associate ministers over the youth department at church listened attentively to my complaints ever since I joined. He was there for me. He counseled me in his office whenever I needed someone to talk to and seemed genuinely concerned about my welfare. I told him all about my rash and how I felt about people calling me ugly, and not feeling loved. He was so understanding and compassionate.

"You're pretty," he said.

"Me, pretty? You're just saying that to make me feel better," I replied.

"No I'm not. You're attractive."

I was stunned. No one—not even my Daddy had ever said I was pretty. He was a minister and he wouldn't lie to me. That day I left out of his office floating, feeling alive.

As time progressed we developed a good rapport and I spent time with his wife Jacqueline (Jackie) and their three children at their home in New Jersey. I was honored to be close to them because they were an esteemed family at church; it made me feel important—like I belonged.

Jackie was slender with the poise of an ostrich. When she entered a room she would capture the attention of everyone because her presence illuminated the space. There was a magnetizing aura about her. And when she led songs in the Radio Broadcast Choir the audience was sometimes moved to tears. She was my role model and I was her best fan.

&&&&&&&

I was in my senior year in High School and making plans for college. I had no goals. For the most part, I lived one day at a time. Although I had Christ in my life, somehow I never thought I'd live very long because I was still not completely happy with living.

My class had taken a trip to Howard University and I was given an opportunity to be admitted there, but my mother said, "No. I can't afford it. I'm not going to send you any money and I'm not going to sign any papers." I wouldn't turn eighteen until December and I couldn't go without her permission.

I believed Mommy didn't want me to go because Wilhelmina didn't go away to college. I brought home better grades, but she got all the attention, encouragement and praise when she brought her report card home. When she was accepted into one of the city universities Mommy made a big deal about it. Although I had little interest in attending the same school, I applied, was accepted; and it was no big deal to Mommy.

I withdrew my second semester and began working at McDonald's across from Madison Square Gardens instead. Later on that year I enrolled in a secretarial training school; graduated in the top one-percent and went on to work as a secretary at a non-profit creative arts center. My employer and supervisors seemed to have a lot of respect for me. They called me "the church girl."

ৡৡৡৡৡৡৡ

I became more engrossed in Bible study and continued to love my family despite the persecution and rejection I felt. I had a new love and hope that would sustain me through the storms. Over time, my itching toned down and I began to heal the more I trusted God. The crusty dark skin, which layered my body for years, was now vanishing like an old blemish, and my disposition began to blossom like fresh yellow sunflowers after a hard winter has passed. No longer was I buried in pity, Christ was my hope.

Within two years after receiving the Holy Ghost my face was clear, I had eyebrows and a glow! Mrs. Maye, a neighbor, said, "Whatever you're doing chil', just keep on doin' it—'cause your skin sho' is clearin' up real good."

Every now and then I would break out and would require a refill on my topical ointment, but nothing like before. My new life in Christ brought inner and outer healing to my body, mind and spirit.

> *For there is hope of a tree, if it be cut down, that it will sprout again, and that the tender branch thereof will not cease. (Job 14:7).*

ૡ-ૡ-ૡ-ૡ-ૡ-ૡ-ૡ

Every now and then Daddy came by the parking lot and hollered up to our window for us to come downstairs. It wasn't particularly easy to get in touch with him, so I was always ecstatic when he called up to us. Usually, Daddy came by to give us some spending money. And he would always remember our birthdays and special occasions.

ও৵ও৵ও৵ও৵ও৵

Elder Johnson, the youth minister who counseled me at church, moved his family to Summerville to start a new church. We kept in touch by mail. Mommy was always suspicious of him writing to me; I thought it was unfounded and unfair. She fussed whenever I got a letter. What was wrong with him caring about me? He's a minister! It seemed Mommy never wanted me to be happy and tried to refuse me of anything that was important to me.

Elder Johnson and his wife invited me to Summerville to visit; to see if I would like it. If I did, they said I could come and live with them and work in the church as a missionary. I considered it, but I wasn't sure about leaving home, my family.

When I visited during the Fourth of July in 1977, I liked Summerville. It was like country to me with all the grass and trees and homes along the streets. But where were the tall buildings and the trash and the decaying tenements? It was incredibly clean. When the Johnson's drove me downtown where many office buildings were located, Elder Johnson said, "This is like New York's Wall Street."—There was no comparison.

Lifted!

The church was small with wooden floors and no pews—just iron folding chairs. It was a far cry from our wall-to-wall plush carpet in New York, but that wasn't an issue to me. When I accompanied Momma to church it was the same thing. But I didn't drive, and getting around Summerville wasn't as easy as getting around in New York City; however, I did prefer the slower pace, less hustle and bustle, and cleanness. I had to mull it over and pray about whether moving to Summerville was what I believed God wanted me to do.

My main concern was that I wanted to move to a place where I was really wanted and could make a positive difference in the lives of others. I could not have been more ready to leave New York; I welcomed the transition. I just wasn't certain if I was prepared to be on my own.

CHAPTER XVI

SUCH SWEET SORROW

One sunny morning in late July, I got up to go to work at the Creative Arts Center. I washed up in the sink and rinsed my feet off in the bathtub. I would have taken a shower but Wilhelmina didn't wash out her bathtub rings and I was drained of cleaning the tub behind her. Wilhelmina had already left for work when my mother got up to use the bathroom that morning. I stood looking in the long hallway mirror making finishing touches to my clothes and hair when my mother said, "Come and clean out this bathtub before you go to work!"

"Those aren't my rings," I replied. "They are Wilhelmina's. I didn't take a bath." I was not in the habit of talking back to my mother, but I determined not to clean out the bathtub that day.

"I didn't ask you whose rings they were; I told you to clean it out!" she commanded.

I breathed deeply and with all the might I could muster said, "I'm not going to clean it out— Wilhelmina dirtied it."

"You what? You what? Who are you talking to like that?"

Lifted!

Mommy came out of the bathroom, went into the kitchen and came back with the broom. She knocked me hard across my back with the stick. It was the last straw.

The water flowed forcefully from the faucet and my eyes as I scrubbed the tub with Comet and a rag. The only peace I had was confidence in knowing that this would be one of the last times I would be cleaning out this bathtub behind anyone else—because I was leaving.

I ran across the street to the pay phone in front of the drug store and called Gayle at work. Sobbing uncontrollably, I explained what had just happened and told her I was leaving. Angrily, and through tears she said, "It's probably best."

> ***In all this Job sinned not, nor charged God foolishly.*** *(Job 1:22).*

ೲೲೲೲೲೲೲೲ

Before making concrete plans I talked it over with my pastor. He approved, and gave me his blessings.

I knew I couldn't leave before Saturday, August 20, 1977, because that was a very important day. Red was getting married and I was in her wedding. However, I did not procrastinate. I left the following day with the yellow Samsonite suitcase her mother gave me.

> *Though thy beginning was small, yet thy latter end should greatly increase. (Job 8:7).*

Lifted!

Vanessa G. Cunningham

PART II

ABUSE

Vanessa G. Cunningham

CHAPTER XVII

GREEN PASTURES

The flight attendant stopped by more than once to ask, "Are you okay? Can I get you anything?" Tissues were all I needed as I cried incessantly—although I tried hard to restrain myself. The airplane ride from New York was unsettling, but it wasn't turbulent due to inclement weather; rather, the brilliant skies shone radiantly through the windowpane. I pulled the stiff rectangular shade down and fixed my head against it to prevent the blazing sun from blinding my stinging red puffy eyes.

I was nineteen when I left home, Harlem--Egypt, the House of Bondage. I was moving to Summerville, greener pastures, the Promised Land, to work for the Lord. But it was not a gratifying exodus.

Just before I was to leave for the airport in a taxi my mother stood on the porch of our building waiting for her friend, Mrs. Easley. They were going to one of Rev. Schambach's tent revival meetings. "Good-bye," Mommy said. That's it! Goodbye. No embrace, no kisses, no blessings.

I was distressed the entire flight. I had a one-way ticket, didn't know when I would be returning, and this was my vile fate.

My disconcerting plane ride was en route to Miami, Florida, where our annual church convocation was being held. There, I planned to meet up with the Johnson's, who had recently moved to Summerville, and travel with them. They invited me to live with them and work in the newly established church there. I was needed to labor in the vineyard.

I was on a mission to win souls to Christ, aid in the "up-building" of the Kingdom of God, and finally discover true serenity. This was a chance for me to escape Egypt and be a missionary for the Lord; I welcomed it.

I remained in Miami for several days sharing a hotel room with some of the young sisters from church, attending workshops, and worship services, before departing to Summerville. I had saved some money and was given a little by a couple of my friend's mom's; but I didn't have an abundant supply. Many of the sisters from home knew I was headed to Summerville, so they threw me a going away party. I would miss my New York church family.

I had not been informed of the travel arrangements to Summerville from Miami. With all that I had going on, it was the least of my concerns. Elder Johnson had told me not to worry about it; they would take care of the plans. All I knew was that I would not be returning to New York, but would be flying from Miami to Summerville. Thus, before I left Manhattan, I shipped my trunk and a couple of boxes directly to Summerville via Greyhound.

৯৯৯৯৯৯৯৯

It was dawn when we left. I was traveling alone with my new pastor. His wife and three children were not returning yet, because they still had some business to take care of in New York and New Jersey. They would be driving back to Summerville in a few days. Accommodations had been for me to stay with one of the church members until his wife and kids returned.

After a brief transport we had to change planes. I had flown a few times prior, but this was my first hot breakfast flight—pancakes and syrup. We sat just beyond the first class section in a row with two seats. I had the window seat; and would occasionally glance out at the endless skies considering God's infinite awesomeness. I also pondered about my new life of joy and tranquility in Summerville.

When the flight attendants retrieved our breakfast trays Pastor Johnson elevated the armrest that separated our seats and laid his head in my lap. I felt rather awkward and apprehensive, but I didn't say anything. It was an uncomfortable predicament to be in; but I guess I should feel honored—I thought.

I was not accustomed to a man laying his head in my lap—ever, but I wasn't going to ask Pastor Johnson to remove his—he was the pastor. Besides, I really didn't know how. I just sat there. Still. Stunned.

> **Surely I would speak to the Almighty, and I desire to reason with God.** *(Job 13:3).*

CHAPTER XVIII

LABORING TO REAP

Early that morning Pastor Johnson and I arrived at the church in the west end of town where his "First Family" was relocating. The apartment I visited a month ago was just a temporary abode. He said they were moving upstairs above the sanctuary because there was much work to do in the church and they wanted to be closer. The place was in total disarray.

Pastor Johnson gave me a brief tour and showed me my bedroom in the back. To get to my room you had to go through the kids' bedroom. He then gave me quick instructions on how I should bring some order to the place. He told me to find some rags, clean and varnish the woodwork, wash the windows, and sweep up the debris, for starters. I had no idea I was going to be left unaccompanied in this building, this strange city—and already put to work, by myself on my first day in town! It was definitely prayer time.

Pastor Johnson headed downtown to work at a major corporation. He said, "I should be back around 4:30 p.m. You will probably want to change into some work clothes."

So how much work was I suppose to complete in that time? I didn't know I was invited to do heavy maintenance like this. This job was too big for me. I thought. Here I was, in a strange city, alone. No phone, no food, no family. There was a refrigerator, but it was bare.

> *When I looked for good, then evil came unto me: and when I waited for light, there came darkness. (Job 30:26).*

ళళళళళళళ

I was more than a little afraid, but determined to make this situation work and be about my Father's business. I had to get busy for the Lord and make things comfortable for the pastor's family so they could do the work that God ordained them to do.

I had no prior experience doing this type of work but I cleaned wood, washed windows, painted shellac on the woodwork, and swept until Pastor Johnson returned from work. I looked a mess! He told me to get ready because Mother Martha Carter was expecting us for dinner. He said I would be spending my nights with her until his family arrived. He gave me a key to the church, a bus ticket, and told me which bus to take to come back in the morning to continue my chores.

This type of work was certainly beyond my imagination; but I guess it was better than being on the foreign field in the outdoors laboring for the Lord. Pastor Johnson seemed satisfied with what I had accomplished. Before we left for Mother Carter's, he showed me how to put up wallpaper in the den. It had a purple and white floral pattern—not what I would have selected. And, he demonstrated to me how I should place 3"x5" blocks of beige ceramic tile in the bathroom the next day.

He was my pastor, and I was taught to obey those that had the rule over me, so I followed his orders. Besides, I thought, this was my reasonable service for room and board; and once things were orderly and comfortable I would get some relief from this type of manual labor. I was persuaded that this was part of my role as a missionary for the Lord, so I dared not complain.

Mother Martha Carter, a devout Christian, lived in the Deluxe West apartment complex—not far from the heart of downtown. She was a maid, cook and housekeeper by profession, and had a beautiful table spread upon our arrival. She had prepared a platter of golden brown fried chicken, white rice, vegetables, and fresh baked homemade biscuits. We also had Lipton iced tea with lemon and pineapple up-side-down cake for dessert.

Mother Carter was a big woman—at least two hundred twenty-five pounds, in her late fifties, with thick, long, black silky hair and eyeglasses. Her complexion was tawny brown. She appeared strong and healthy, and just as kind and compassionate as she was firm.

Mother Carter didn't have any children of her own but was just as lovable a mother one could find anywhere, and sincere. She enjoyed making dinner for her pastor and considered it a privilege to have him over and serve him. After dinner, Pastor Johnson left and Mother Carter and I got better acquainted.

"How did you come to know the Johnson's?" she asked, while we cleaned up the kitchen.

"We were all members of the same church in New York and he was one of the associate pastors to the youth," I replied.

Lifted!

"Are you closer to Elder Johnson or Sister Johnson?" she asked inquisitively.

"Both," I said. "I spent time with them at their home in New Jersey, and at church he would counsel me. Sister Johnson is one of the people I admire most in the world. She sang in the radio choir with conviction. I was persuaded and inspired by every note."

"Yes, she really does sing beautifully. Like a bird," she responded.

"When they were commissioned to come to Summerville to start a church we wrote each other often and they invited me to come and work in the church," I added. We dressed for bed, said our prayers, and I thanked Mother Carter for the good meal and for allowing me to stay with her.

ॐॐॐॐॐॐॐ

My room was comfortable, and the bed warm. The gorgeous patchwork quilt reminded me of being down south in North Carolina. Mother Carter's mother had sewn the quilt entirely with her hands. I thought, I don't mind staying here one bit. Thank you, Jesus.

After boarding the 103 Broadway bus westbound that morning, I found my way back to the empty white wooden church on the corner of

Fifty-first Street and West End Avenue. I opened the church door and went upstairs to commence my toiling. I concluded in my mind that this must work out. This was my new home. I had nothing else. I could not go back. Things would get better. This was the hardest part.

৯৯৯৯৯৯৯

It was not fun putting up wallpaper and laying tile alone, but the more I worked and beheld the fruits of my labor the better I felt. I was doing something worthwhile that was appreciated.

Pastor Johnson arrived home that afternoon with a meal from a fast food seafood restaurant. I was unfamiliar with the name of the restaurant and had never experienced the peculiar taste before. It was rather uncommon for me to eat chicken planks and fish that was battered and fried the same. And the crumbs around the fries—were they to be eaten?

৯৯৯৯৯৯৯

Pastor Johnson changed out of his suit into some old clothes and started helping me with the floor and walls. I was really beat and ready to retire for the day, but I was expected to continue working so I did. The place was beginning to look habitable. He was pleased and I was impressed at what I had accomplished in two days. It was getting late; it was time for me to be getting back to Mother Carter's. When Pastor Johnson asked, "Are you ready to go?" I did not hesitate.

Pastor Johnson said, "I'm going to take my bath first, then you can take yours." As always, I concurred. And when he got out, he said, "You can use my water." I was not used to taking a bath in someone else's bath water; we had plenty of hot running water in the projects. Nor did I want to wash in anyone else's tub if they had not cleaned it out yet; but I did not disagree with him. I just did as I was told.

I got in the water and began to wash. A couple of times Pastor Johnson came in the bathroom while I was washing. There was no lock on the bathroom door nor a shower curtain or doors to hide behind.

He was dark, thin, well-groomed and of average height; eleven or twelve years my senior— my "Father in the Gospel." He had dressed and began shaving in the mirror while I was in the tub. And he acted as if there was nothing wrong with it—as if it was okay—as if it was normal for him to be in there with me.

I wasn't comfortable, but I did nothing, said nothing. When he left the room I hurriedly got out of the tub and put on my yellow and white terry cloth robe and rushed toward my bedroom. I got dressed and he escorted me to Mother Carter's. We walked several blocks and talked until the bus came.

> *Who can bring a clean thing out of an unclean? Not one. (Job 14:4).*

CHAPTER XIX

PLOTTING TO RAPE

The next day was the same routine. I worked hard all day to make things pleasant for Pastor Johnson's family, who would be arriving in a few days, and he pitched in to help when he came home from work. However, when he arrived home this afternoon, he took a bath, and left the water for me—but he didn't come into the bathroom to shave like he did the day before. I was relieved. Maybe he had thought about it and realized it was inappropriate behavior. I was grateful.

Pastor Johnson was rather quiet in his room and I didn't want to disturb him in the event he was praying or meditating, so I robed myself and crept out of the bathroom. Before I could swiftly pass by his bedroom, which was about three feet away from the bathroom, he snatched me inside his bedroom and threw me down on the mattress and box spring. He had placed a mirror on the ceiling above the bed to surprise his wife, but he didn't wait for her.

Pastor Johnson held my legs high in the air; my head was pinned against the wall. He was like an evil madman—a person I didn't know. I'd only known him to be gentle and caring.

He put Vaseline on his penis and in my rectum. I had no inkling of what to expect. I could not believe what was happening. What was he doing? Why?

I squirmed and pleaded with him to let me go to no avail. He behaved as if he wasn't even listening to me—like it didn't matter what I said. He jabbed himself into my anus and thrust himself into me hard and then harder several times. The trauma was unimaginable. He kept slapping my buttocks and badgering me saying, "Say I'm the best! Say I'm the best!" I cried hysterically. "Ow! Stop! What are you doing? You're hurting me! Ow! You're the best! You're the best!" But he didn't stop until he was ready—until he was finished.

> *Make me to know my transgression and my sin. For this is a heinous crime; yea, it is an iniquity to be punished by the judges. (Job 13:23b; 31:11).*

"Are you okay?" he questioned, as I lay there still, unable to move. This was a nightmare and I would be waking up soon, I hoped.

I bled. I hurt. I could not sit down. I could not go to the bathroom. I was distraught, perplexed, confused, and distracted. But I tried to behave as if I was all right when he dropped me off at Mother Carter's that night.

> *Man that is born of a woman is of few days, and full of trouble. He cometh forth like a flower, and is cut down: he fleeth also as a shadow, and continueth not. (Job 14:1-2).*

ତ୬ତ୬ତ୬ତ୬ତ୬ତ୬ତ୬

I couldn't tell Mother Carter. I knew no one else there. I couldn't tell anyone in New York. Who would believe me?

He was my friend, counselor, pastor, and "Father in the Gospel. I didn't want to hurt him. I didn't want to get him in trouble. He had helped me over the years and put a roof over my head.

I never swore because the Bible says, "Swear not at all," but Pastor Johnson made me swear to my grave that I would tell no one—especially not his wife. I promised. I told no one.

> *My transgression is sealed up in a bag, and thou sewest up mine iniquity.* *(Job 14:17).*

୨◦୨◦୨◦୨◦୨◦୨◦୨◦୨

When Sister Johnson arrived home a few days later with the kids, her new residence above the church was fit for habitation. I was relieved she was home, but I didn't feel the same in her company. I felt ashamed and guilty—like I had betrayed her. Although in my heart of hearts I didn't believe that I had done anything wrong. I had only tried to leave an uncomfortable environment to start life anew and work for the Lord. I just wanted to serve Jesus in the beauty of holiness and win souls to Christ.

୨◦୨◦୨◦୨◦୨◦୨◦୨◦୨

My back was against a wall. Which was the lesser of the two evils? Do I stay in Summerville or go back to New York?

> *If I wait, the grave is mine house: I have made my bed in the darkness. I have said to corruption, Thou art my father: to the worm, Thou art my*

98

mother, and my sister. And where is now my hope? As for my hope, who shall see it? (Job 17:13-15).

CHAPTER XX

USED AND CONFUSED

A few days passed. Pastor and Sister Johnson were in their bedroom, the kids were playing in their room, and I was settled in my rose colored room with a twin bed, a nightstand and lamp. My room had a gray metal closet for my belongings and, beside it, a window that faced north with a beige shade for the morning sun. The tension and internal stress I felt were veiled. Everything appeared fine. But daily, I hurt inwardly.

I had looked forward to bonding more with Sister Johnson and learning from her. She was such a lady, feminine, and gentle. I looked up to her and cared dearly for her. She was virtuous in my eyes. She told me to call her "Jackie," but I preferred calling her Sister Johnson out of respect for her position. I didn't want the other saints to think it was acceptable for them to call her by her first name so I tried to set an example.

Sister Johnson and I got along well and enjoyed doing things together. I was like her personal assistant. She relied on me and I considered myself blessed to be worthy of the vocation.

Lifted!

One night while I was in bed reading Pastor Johnson came into my bedroom wearing only a red and black terry cloth wrap with a wide black stripe. That was the first time I'd ever glanced upon one before because my Daddy never wore one. In our house we barely had enough towels and washcloths to go around. We couldn't afford such unessential luxuries.

In wide-eyed disbelief I looked at him as he flipped open the wrap and stood near the door, erect, and full of lust, saying nothing. Then he left.

When I awakened the next day I felt as if I had been bad, as if I had sinned. I felt isolated, dirty and full of grief. But I could tell no one.

ণ্ডণ্ডণ্ডণ্ডণ্ডণ্ডণ্ড

Habitually, Pastor Johnson would check on the kids, turn out their light and come into my room. I was relieved when Sister Johnson read them a book, kissed them goodnight and turned out their light. I felt safer.

Occasionally Pastor Johnson stood standing in my door talking to me when he knew the kids weren't asleep yet, or if he thought it too risky to come closer. Sister Johnson came looking for him when she thought he'd taken too long. It was such an awkward position to be in. I hated him doing that to me. The whole matter made me sick—yet he had a nonchalant attitude about its affects on anyone.

Like clockwork, at bedtime Pastor Johnson would enter my room with just a robe or his wrap on and would put his forefinger to his mouth saying, "Shhh." His facial expressions were frightening—like I had better be quiet and obey him or suffer the consequences of his wrath. He appeared as though his appetite could not be quenched as he looked at me straight in the eyes and drew nigh to me. "Touch it," he said.

"I don't want to," I retorted softly.

"Rub it," he warned with his lips stuck out as if all power on earth was in his hands.

Quietly, I squirmed and pleaded, "I don't want to."

"Put it in your mouth," he ordered.

His wife was in their bedroom steps away. I was frightened of them both.

Is there iniquity in my tongue? Cannot my taste discern perverse things? Let that day be darkness; let not God regard it from above, neither let the light shine upon it.

Lifted!

Let darkness and the shadow of death stain it; let a cloud dwell upon it; let the blackness of the day terrify it. As for that night, let darkness seize upon it; let it not be joined unto the days of the year; let it not come into the number of the months. (Job 6:30; 3:4-6).

৩১৯৩১৯৩১৯৩১৯

I performed more chores than I had ever dreamed of, but it was all to the glory of God, for the "up-building" of the Kingdom of God, I kept telling myself to try to eradicate the guilt I bore.

I didn't love him. I didn't want him. Why would he not leave me alone?

৩১৯৩১৯৩১৯৩১৯

My trunk and boxes arrived so Pastor Johnson drove me to pick them up. While riding in the car he took my hand and placed it on his private. "Zip it down," he said. I did. Then he took himself out and told me to put my head in his lap. I did. As trucks and buses passed by he pushed my head down and held it there. I was repulsed and could not breathe.

Pastor Johnson always wanted to drive me wherever I needed to go. Sometimes his wife volunteered and it was more feasible for her to drive me, but he wouldn't let her. He always told her to take care of the kids. And she walked his chalk line. Obedient, submissive, and subservient—that was the role of the women in our church.

Once I thought Pastor Johnson was going to have a heart attack or die right on the spot when he parked the car in a cloistered area. His eyes ballooned and turned bloodshot red as if they were going to shoot out like bullets from a gun. I had no idea where we were, although sometimes I know he drove to Indiana. He assured me everything was fine.

"I don't like this," I said.

"Whew!" he said, shaking his head as if it would bring him relief.

"What's the matter? What's wrong?" I asked. I was afraid. He shook his head again, but this time in wonderment, and gathered himself together. I'd hoped he was frightened enough to renounce these scandalous activities, but it was not over.

*I should have been as though I
had not been; I should have been*

> *carried from the womb to the grave. If I be wicked, woe unto me; and if I be righteous, yet will I not lift up my head. (Job 10:19, 15a).*

৯৯৯৯৯৯৯৯

I felt used and overwhelmed. I was Hazel, and I did not like it. The measure of the domestic tasks I did far exceeded expenses for room and board— and that's not what I came to do. I came to work for the Lord. It was time for me to start looking for a job so I could pay my way and escape.

৯৯৯৯৯৯৯৯

After a few weeks I was hired as a clerk typist at Summerville Fire & Casualty Company downtown. Pastor Johnson and I rode the bus together each morning and met at the bus stop to return most afternoons. We both worked in the same building and sometimes met for lunch. I felt proud that my pastor wanted to have lunch with me. But he usually wanted to take me to some secluded spot so that I could take care of him. I hated feeling obligated to satisfy him like that; but when I dissented he became angry and enraged at my protest. So I obeyed.

While on my new job my co-workers were so intrigued by my northern linguistics that they would take me around like a circus animal doing "show and tell" and ask me to say "coffee."

"Coffee," I said, to a whirl of laughter.

"Say New York."

"New York," I'd reiterate.

"Listen to her accent," they'd bellow out as if I were from an unknown land.

"I don't have an accent. You all have accents."

"You all! You all! Listen to her. You all! We don't say 'you all' here. We say "y'all."

"What?" I laughed. "It's 'you all'."

For months my co-workers had me echoing words like Boston, dog, and soda (which they called pop). And although I'd repeat it over and over again—they would still say, "Say that again."

৯৯৯৯৯৯৯৯

Wilhelmina and I corresponded by mail and, as a present, I sent her a poster that read, "Absence Makes the Heart Grow Fonder." She seemed to grow more warmhearted toward me since I was away. On occasion, I made long distance calls to my family and special friends; but I couldn't afford to do it too often. When I spoke to my Mommy, the communication was somewhat strained but we were both trying hard not to let it be so.

CHAPTER XXI

GRIEVED AND DECEIVED

It was incestuous for Pastor Johnson to bother me. He was my "Father in the Gospel," my pastor—but it didn't seem to quite matter to him. He didn't discontinue his acts toward me.

He kept preaching and teaching and I continued my service in the church as Sunday school superintendent, Sunday school teacher, church secretary, radio broadcast announcer, choir director, and altar worker. Wherever and whatever capacity I was needed to serve in—I did, without hesitation. And as I served, I suffered.

Service was held at least twice on Sundays, and Bible study, prayer and choir rehearsal during the week. Oftentimes we had nightly revival services that were either carried out by Pastor Johnson or an out-of-town evangelist whom we housed. When we had guests I got a respite from the sexual harassment. I always wanted the visiting ministers to extend their stay because Pastor Johnson was reluctant to bother me then.

Lifted!

৯৯৯৯৯৯৯৯

I remained steadfast in prayer—moaning, groaning, repenting and begging God to help me out of this mire. I abhorred this Isle of Patmos, and did not know how to make it to shore. I only wanted to love and be loved the way Christ intended. I wanted to be righteous, holy, and pure.

> *Oh that I might have my request; and that God would grant me the thing that I long for! Behold, I cry out of wrong, but I am not heard: I cry aloud, but there is no judgment. Oh that my words were now written! Oh that they were printed in a book! That they were graven with an iron pen and lead in the rock for ever!* (Job 6:8; 19:7, 23-24).

৯৯৯৯৯৯৯৯

Never did I think I would go to hell for what I was doing because I was obeying God's minister—His servant in charge of my soul. I was trying to please him so that he would not be mad at me. Never did I desire him or try to seduce him—

never! But at times I felt like a Pentecostal prostitute—only I wasn't getting paid. Pastor Johnson never showered me with gifts as remuneration for my services or to keep me coming back. I wanted nothing and I got nothing. My subservience to him was only to avoid his displeasure, to stay on his good side, so that he would continue to love me as he said he did.

> *Shall mortal man be more just than God? Shall a man be more pure than his Maker? (Job 4:17).*

ঌঌঌঌঌঌঌ

Often, I bought a Hallmark card and left it where I knew Sister Johnson would soon find it. I could spend my vacation and last dime in a card store. I never rushed when I was selecting a card for someone because it had to say exactly what my heart was speaking. It had to be a Hallmark, because the receiver had to know that I was sending them only the very best.

At times I would slip Sister Johnson a card under her bedroom door when I knew she was in there alone and could read it pensively. I would sign it, "With all my heart." She always loved my cards and would let me know how much they meant to her.

The etching on the cards was not quite as crucial as the words, but the design had to fit the occasion. Most of the time the cards were three-fold watercolors. And they were always very wordy. Sometimes they expressed my gratitude, some were apologetic, and at other times they imparted my helplessness and desire for protection. I needed the cards to say what I could not say myself. I hoped she would pick up the subtleties and rescue me.

On occasion I'd get a blank note and write my own words when I just couldn't seem to find the exact words to express my sentiments at that particular time. I wrote:

> *Dear Sister Johnson,*
>
> *Ever since the day I first heard you singing, "Hold on, you shall receive a reward from the Lord," I've admired you. You sang with such fervor and conviction that immediately I was persuaded to believe.*
>
> *And when God permitted me to spend time with you at your home and get to know you personally I felt so honored and blessed. You were busy*

with your children, but still attentive to me.

I look up to you, Sister Johnson, as a mentor and a Christian role model. And I have deep respect for you. I wish more people were like you—sincere, trusting and wise. You have a meek and quiet spirit—but yet you are strong.

I wish I were strong like you instead of timid and insecure. And I wish I had your boldness to stand my ground and not be swayed. Too often I try to please people and buy their love. I don't want to be like this, but it's all I know. And if I turn people down or don't do what they expect of me they will be mad at me or they won't like me.

Please pray for me, Sister Johnson, that God will help me to be stronger so that I will please Him rather than man.

God truly favored me when he brought you into my life. I love you.

With all my love,

Vonnette

Lifted!

Sometimes I felt Sister Johnson knew her husband was bothering me but refused to believe it. She often told me, "Vonnette, you need to learn to say no." I think she chose to believe otherwise because she was afraid of the truth, wanted to trust him, and didn't want to lose him. She also wanted to maintain her status. According to our doctrine she could not marry again unless he died, so she chose an ostrich-like state because it was her security.

Meanwhile, because of the emotional baggage and weight I carried, I died daily from the burden of sin and I suffocated and drowned in guilt quicksand.

> *My soul is weary of my life; I will leave my complaint upon myself; I will speak in the bitterness of my soul. I will say unto God, Do not condemn me; show me whereof thou contendest with me. (Job 10:1-2).*

At times I was angry with Sister Johnson because I couldn't see how she could be so close to

God, so spiritual—yet so blind about what her husband was doing to me, to us. I could stand and fight if she helped me, but I could not contest him alone.

Words went unspoken, but there was a bond between us that assured me she could feel my pain when I rolled under the bench holding my aching stomach and travailing in prayer after the benediction was given. We cried together, and we hugged and held each other, but we said nothing.

> *But his flesh upon him shall have pain, and his soul within him shall mourn. I went mourning without the sun: I stood up, and I cried in the congregation. (Job 14:22; 30:28).*

৵৵৵৵৵৵৵৵

It was absolutely intolerable to live in that room above the church and have my pastor visit me night after night seeking thrills. I asked Mother Carter if I could pay her for room and board and live with her. She had no idea why the sudden decision, but she didn't question me for an explanation. She said, "Vonnette, I will be glad to have you. You are like the daughter I never had."

I thanked her and I thanked God for my new home.

᳜᳜᳜᳜᳜᳜᳜ᷧᷧᷧᷧᷧᷧᷧ

Robed in fine attire, Pastor Johnson stood flat-footed and tall and preached a thunderous sermon:

> *Fornication and adultery is sin, and all liars will have their part in the lake that burns with fire and brimstone! Hallelujah! Glory to God! Can I get an Amen?*
>
> *You must be born again of the water and of the Spirit to enter the Kingdom of God. There, He will say, "Well done, my good and faithful servant." If you want Him to say well done, stand to your feet and come to Jesus. Repent of your sins and make Jesus your personal savior.*
>
> *Come to Jesus. Come to Jesus and He will cleanse you from all of your sins and make you whole. You won't look the same. You won't feel the same. And you won't do the things*

*you used to do. He will change
you. Come to Jesus right now.*

ততততততত

He would then come down from the pulpit and
greet the members and guests who were lined up
because they wanted him specifically to pray for a
personal need or because they were so enthralled
over the sermon. They told Pastor Johnson that he
really preached, that they got so much out of the
sermon, and that the sermon was meant just for
them.

Pastor   Johnson   didn't   discourage   the
worshippers from flocking to him because he was
there for them. He was a good listener and
extended himself to all. However, on occasion,
when he preached so hard that his clothes were
soaked from perspiration, he wanted to get into dry
clothes first.

Most times, Pastor Johnson was eager to take
me home when Mother Carter didn't come back
for evening worship. When a member offered to
give me a ride, Pastor Johnson would say that he
had to go out anyway to pick something up in that
area. When Sister Johnson volunteered to drop
me off, he would not let her. He told her to get the
kids ready for bed. And when someone else

needed a ride in the direction I was going Pastor
Johnson insisted that he drop us all off. Of course,
I was always the last stop. I longed for dear old
Harlem and all its pollution and debris.

> *Oh that my grief were thoroughly
> weighed, and my calamity laid in
> the balances together!* *(Job 6:2).*

৩৯৩৯৩৯৩৯৩৯

Once, Pastor Johnson walked seven blocks to
Mother Carter's house to visit me on his lunch
hour while she was at work and I was home sick.
He called me before he left his office to say he was
on his way. I was glad for the forewarning,
because I had time to dress, but I really didn't need
him to come by. He didn't even care that I wasn't
feeling well.

Pastor Johnson knocked on the door; I looked
out the peephole and let him in. Within no time
he had me on the floor in Mother Carter's living
room kissing me and pulling himself out.
Suddenly, the doorbell rang and he jumped to his
feet and peeked out the window to see who it
might be. It was Sister Johnson! He didn't have
time to run upstairs or anything, so he hid in the
living room.

I opened the door to let Sister Johnson in and she said, "I came by to see how you were feeling." At that time I felt sicker than I ever had, but I said that I was coming along. The pit of my stomach was heavy and I felt so guilty and ashamed. I could have just died.

> *Is not destruction to the wicked?*
> *And a strange punishment to the*
> *workers of iniquity? (Job 31:3).*

ೲೲೲೲೲೲೲ

I don't know if Sister Johnson suspected that someone else was in the apartment or not, but I sensed that she did. She didn't even sit down at the kitchen table with me. She just said, "I just wanted to see how you were doing." And she left. It seemed I didn't breathe the entire short time she was there. And I wasn't much relieved after she left. I was full of woe, but Pastor Johnson seemed little concerned about me. He just wanted to make a clean escape himself. I have never forgotten how I felt that day.

> *If a man die, shall he live again?*
> *All the days of my appointed*

*time will I wait, till my change
come. (Job 14:14).*

ॐॐॐॐॐॐॐ

So often Pastor Johnson went to great lengths
and took dangerous, selfish risks without regard for
anyone else. He didn't even consider the sanctity
of Mother Carter's home. It scared me! What
about his conscience? What about his ministry?
The public? His children?

On occasion, Pastor Johnson made
recommendations to me about what apparel I
should wear from my wardrobe and what I should
not wear beneath it. And when he would see me
he would say, "Vonnette, pull up your dress," as
he pointed his index finger to demonstrate that I
should turn in a circle. "Turn around," he said.
And at times he would fondle me.

CHAPTER XXII

SCORNED

About two months after I was hired, Thomas Gray, a young black man around my age, started working in the same claims department. Thomas also attended a Pentecostal church. He was handsomely dressed; wore braces; and had beautiful soft-looking skin that made him healthy-looking. Thomas had an even-tone medium-brown complexion, and a cute baby face, with big brown eyes and long black eyelashes. Thomas was short and a little overweight, but his soft, shipshape black wavy hair and jovial personality hid any would-be flaws.

All the girls tried to fix us up, but I was a little shy. I hadn't dated too many boys before. As time passed and we got pretty acquainted, Thomas and I would walk to his church during lunchtime and he'd play the organ or piano. We harmonized duets and sang solos unto the Lord. Thomas relished being the center of attention, which he was accustomed to, since he was raised as an only child. He was lighthearted, humorous, and fun to be with.

Lifted!

Pastor Johnson didn't like Thomas absorbing my time—his time. He tried to discourage the relationship and appeared jealous at times; but Thomas and I found pleasure in each other's company. It was easy to tell, when he introduced me to his friends, that he was impressed by the fact that I was a New Yorker.

Thomas played the organ or piano for his choir and would occasionally direct. I sometimes visited his church and he visited mine. It was more difficult for me to get away since I had a lot of responsibilities to carry out at my church. I liked Thomas' outgoing spirit; however, I wasn't ready for a serious relationship with him because I thought he was a little immature; but I liked that he liked me.

Thomas helped to drive when the Johnson's and I traveled to visit our families in New York and New Jersey, during Christmas that year. Thomas was excited about going to New York and it was a blessing that he was along, because it began to snow heavily during our sixteen-hour road trip. After we pulled over to the shoulder to change drivers we realized that we were stuck in the snow. Thomas did not hesitate to volunteer to get out and push the car onto the highway.

My family liked Thomas immediately. He seemed to fit right in. Christmas time at our home was just like Thanksgiving—family time in the Covington household. Everyone was glad to see everyone. For Christmas, our family fixed and ate turkey and dressing, ham, collard greens, stringed beans, potato salad, macaroni and cheese, cranberry sauce, rice and gravy. Cousin Minnie usually baked the cakes, and Mommy made the best sweet potato pies on earth. She made about a dozen pies that didn't last much longer than a day.

ৡ৵ৡ৵ৡ৵ৡ৵

Several months passed and, emotionally, I could no longer endure what was happening to me in Summerville. I talked myself into believing that moving back was what I needed to do. When I visited my family in New York during Christmas they received me warmly and I had a wonderful time. If I move back home I can bond with my mother and things will be better than they are in Summerville.

I resigned from work giving the company a two-week notice. Some of the girls in the office took me to lunch and gave me going away gifts. They gave me a lovely brown, gold and beige satin derby scarf with an array of horses printed throughout the border and a gray and white stuffed animal. They said, "This is so you will always remember us. It's an elephant, because elephants never forget."

The church presented me with a framed certificate. It read:

SERVICE AWARD
PRESENTED
TO

Vonnette Covington

WITH LOVE
IN DEEP APPRECIATION
FOR
DEPENDABILITY AND LOYALTY.

It was signed by Pastor Johnson and dated May 18, 1978.

৯৯৯৯৯৯৯৯

I was home for two months before I determined that staying in New York was the greater of the two evils. When I'd visited I enjoyed myself so well and felt so wanted that I thought it was worthwhile and beneficial to move back. But quickly I realized that visiting during vacations and residing permanently was paradoxical. I felt lonely in that big city and I didn't feel the familial compassion I did when I came for short spans. I was not happy—so I returned to Summerville with all my worldly possessions, because I felt more loved there.

I convinced myself that Pastor Johnson was no longer going to bother me because he liked the help I provided around the church and he didn't want me to move away again.

> *Behold, I go forward, but He is not there; and backward, but I cannot perceive Him; On the left hand, where He doth work, but I cannot behold Him: He hideth himself on the right hand, that I cannot see Him: But He knoweth the way that I take: when He hath tried me, I shall come forth as gold. (Job 23:8-10).*

ഐഐഐഐഐഐ

Immediately I was hired as a secretary in the investment department of Summerville Corporation with better pay, since I'd left a good record. I enjoyed my job immensely. I had three immediate bosses who were sticklers for accuracy—but I didn't complain because I knew it would only help me in the long run to pay attention to detail and produce quality work. We got along extremely well.

Mother Carter had changed her membership and joined another body but we still remained close. I roomed with Lisa, one of the sister's from church. Lisa had her own house, which was walking distance from the church.

ఴఴఴఴఴఴఴ

Pastor Johnson was still after me and would occasionally come by Lisa's to walk with me to the bus stop in the mornings to go to work. Although I enjoyed his company, I could never adjust to the ordeal. Sometimes he came by Lisa's when we weren't walking to the bus stop. I hated it, and could be tormented no longer. I was suffocating and without peace. Jimmy Swaggart and Jim Bakker were all over the media for bringing a reproach against the cloth, and Pastor Johnson was doing the same surreptitiously—and I was involved.

More than a year had passed and Thomas and I continued to date. Thomas began sensing that Pastor Johnson was rather protective of me. I shrugged it off. Thomas said, "Your pastor doesn't want us together because he wants you for himself. He is after you." I denied it.

*If I justify myself, mine own
mouth shall condemn me: If I say
I am perfect, it shall also prove
me perverse. (Job 9:20).*

৵৵৵৵৵৵৵৵

I liked the fact that Thomas was in Pastor
Johnson's way. As long as I dated Thomas I had
protection from my pastor. Occasionally,
however, Pastor Johnson became extremely angry
and adamant. He said to me, "Are you sure
Thomas is not gay?" Thomas and I had not been
sexually involved. We weren't supposed to be.
Why was Pastor Johnson making such inferences?

Thomas told me that he loved me, and I told
him the same. We talked about marriage on
occasion; but I was a little afraid of that subject.
When I married I wanted it to be forever and ever,
Amen. I didn't think Thomas was quite ready for
that.

Christmas, 1979, was really special and
memorable. Thomas and I splurged on each
other. He bought me a fur hat and scarf and I
bought him some really nice gifts that I wrapped
and decorated with Hershey's chocolate kisses.

Thomas and I fell into sin for the first time ever,
January 1980. We used no protection. It wasn't

planned. I recall how we waited to see if I got my period late that month. Well something happened, but it was lighter than normal. We thought we were safe; however when I visited over his family's house I could not stay awake to watch the *Exorcist* on television. I then began to have morning sickness. I told Thomas that I thought I was pregnant, and he told me that he did not want me to have it. I had a pregnancy test, and it came back positive. What was I to do?

I thought about the people in my church and his church and what I was supposed to stand for. I was ashamed. I made plans to get rid of it, but I couldn't go through with it because I loved God, Thomas, and the baby that was in me.

Never had I felt more alone than I did one dreadfully cold Monday evening when Thomas and I met at his church to tell his pastor that we had sinned and that I was pregnant. The weatherman had said to stay in if at all possible. Ice was all over the ground and as the winds blew the loose snow was blinding.

I was six weeks pregnant when Thomas completely denied being the father of my unborn child to his pastor. He said to his pastor, "I am not sure the baby is mine—it could be Pastor Johnson's." It was incredulous, inconceivable, and beyond comprehension. I was speechless, humiliated, appalled. I had fallen in love with Thomas, and this was my reward? He had never even told me that he had any doubt. He had me out in left field. He knew it was his baby! How could he lie like that about me to his pastor? What did I do to him to deserve this treatment? How could he not protect me? How could he be so selfish? Was I such a terrible person? I knew that it was not Pastor Johnson's; there was no question about it.

Grief-stricken, I looked Thomas straight in the eyes as we sat in his pastor's office and I said, "Thomas, you know and I know that this baby I am carrying is yours." With my right hand raised I proclaimed, "My witness is in heaven and my record is on high." His pastor seemed to delight in the juicy gossip. He believed Thomas, and made a motion to call our Bishop in New York.

Thomas' pastor called in a deacon as a witness, who happened to be Thomas' uncle, and asked us to repeat what we had just said. I gathered whatever strength I had left in me and walked across the rug to the door with my head in the air, and left.

There is no darkness, nor shadow
of death, where the workers of

iniquity may hide themselves.
(Job 34:22).

I was hysterical. What do I do now? I went to the telephone to call Sister Johnson to tell her what had just happened. She tried to calm me. Thomas walked pass me, and left me stranded at his church. What else could go wrong? I called one of the sister's from our church; who came out in the frosty weather to pick me up and take me home. It was one of the longest, saddest nights of my entire life.

> *Then Job answered the Lord, and said, Behold, I am vile; what shall I answer thee? I will lay mine hand upon my mouth. Wherefore I abhor myself and repent in dust and ashes. (Job 40:3-4; 42:6).*

ൟൟൟൟൟൟ

Because I had sinned and brought a reproach against the church Pastor Johnson "sat me down." He said, "I don't want to do this, but I have to because I don't want to show favoritism. If I let you get by, then I will have to let others get by."

So I could no longer serve in the church—sit only. He could get up in the pulpit and preach, to me, and the congregation, but I could do nothing but show up and give my tithes and offerings. It was hard; it was humbling; it was humiliating.

> *Behold, happy is the man whom God correcteth: therefore despise not thou the chastening of the Almighty. (Job 5:17).*

ৼৼৼৼৼৼৼৼ

Well, I sat. And I sat. And an evangelist came to town to run a revival, which lasted all week. One night he preached a dynamic sermon about crossing over the Jordan River, and then he called for a special faith offering:

> *I want everyone in here to pull out a special faith offering of fifty-dollars. Now, I know some of you might say you don't have it to spare. Well, that's what makes it a faith offering. When you make a sacrifice to give—it is by faith. And whatsoever you ask in faith, believing, it shall be done unto you.*

> *Now, if you don't have the*
> *faith, don't give. I only want*
> *true believers to give in this*
> *offering. Now, faith is the*
> *substance of things hoped for*
> *and the evidence of things not*
> *seen. So, according to your*
> *faith give as unto the Lord.*

I was broke, and giving fifty-dollars was going to be a true sacrifice. But I felt as close to God at that time as I ever had and I needed a miracle. I stood in line with my gift and asked Him to forgive me and bless me.

> *If thou return to the Almighty,*
> *thou shalt be built up, thou shalt*
> *put away iniquity far from thy*
> *tabernacles. And thou shalt*
> *know that thy tabernacle shall be*
> *in peace; and thou shalt visit thy*
> *habitation, and shalt not sin.*
> *(Job 22:23; 5:24).*

৯৯৯৯৯৯৯

I sat—until one Sunday morning the Holy Ghost fell on me like a whirlwind. I was on my feet shouting and dancing in my pregnant state. I had been sitting and meditating about Job and how his friends criticized him and accused him of wrongdoing. I thought about how Job trusted God and maintained his integrity in the face of insurmountable foes. My faith increased, my spirit was lifted, and I was revived.

Some of the missionaries got up from their seats and came over to me. They began rebuking me saying, "Sit down! Sit down! You don't have nothin'. Sit down!"

But I would not sit down.

CHAPTER XXIII

DELIVERED AND LIFTED!

I raised my hands and waved them toward heaven proclaiming my liberty. My mind no longer felt clouded and strained. I rejoiced and cried because I was rejuvenated, and because I knew I did have something. I got a breakthrough! What those sisters were saying mattered not to me. I was delivered!

> *Then Job answered the Lord, and said, I know that thou canst do every thing, and that no thought can be withholden from thee. When men are cast down, then thou shalt say, There is lifting up; and He shall save the humble person. He shall deliver the island of the innocent: and it is delivered by the pureness of thine hands. He shall deliver thee in six troubles: yea, in seven there shall no evil touch thee. (Job 42:1-2; 22:29-30; 5:19).*

From that moment, my mind was renewed and elevated. I was refreshed. I felt like I had been released from prison and was bound no more— except for the Promised Land. I was so thankful to God—

> **Which doeth great things past finding out; yea, and wonders without number.** *(Job 9:10).*

৵৽৵৽৵৽৵৽

I believed, still, that Pastor Johnson wanted me in his life the same way; but I finally had the strength and power to walk away and not return. I had a new determination, because I knew that God knew my heart. He knows who I am better than I know myself. I didn't believe that God had brought me this far to leave me because His Word said that He would never leave me neither forsake me.

I sought professional counseling and learned that it doesn't matter how much authority, or power someone has—many times you can choose not to let anyone control you, use you, or take advantage of you. The healing starts within one's mind. If we give our all to Christ, He will keep us in perfect peace and He will keep that which we have committed unto Him against the evil one.

> ***What is man, that thou shouldest magnify him? And that thou shouldest set thine heart upon him?*** *(Job 7:17).*

৯৯৯৯৯৯৯

I asked the Lord to take control of my mind. I told Him that I wanted to have the mind of Christ. I changed my membership to another church in Summerville and over the years learned that God is too great for me to live among the lowly. In Christ, I am an "overcomer!" Through Christ, I can do all things that strengthen me; and I am more than a conqueror! I am free because God says I am free; and whom the Lord sets free is truly free indeed!

Defining myself in Christ, loving myself, and setting boundaries is what I've learned to do. I gave my son to the Lord when he was in my womb, raised him as a single parent, and now he is saved and working for the Lord. God brought us through many, many storms. He is yet faithful. There is none like Him in all the earth and none can be compared to Him.

Because of my tests and trials I have a relationship with God that is indescribable and inexpressible. I really know who He is. I know what true love is and I know the true meaning of forgiveness.

If a man dies—through Christ—he shall live again!

> *And the Lord turned the captivity of Job, when he prayed for his friends: also the Lord gave Job twice as much as he had before. (Job 42:10).*

ଡ଼ଡ଼ଡ଼ଡ଼ଡ଼ଡ଼ଡ଼

Daddy has been happily remarried for nearly two decades. Mommy never remarried—but she and I are very close now. Gayle, Ulysses and Wilhelmina's families are doing well. Dwayne still lives at home with Mommy.

And, as for me, Vonnette, I believe I am truly living for the first time because I know in whom I believe and I am persuaded that He will keep that which I have committed unto Him against that day. By God's grace, I have been *lifted!*

Lifted!

So the Lord blessed the latter end of Job more than his beginning. . .
(Job 42:12a).

Vanessa G. Cunningham

About the Author

Vanessa G. Cunningham, 44, was born in the heart of Harlem in New York City. At an early age she gave her life to Christ. Besides Vanessa's love for the Word of God, she has a deep affection for writing.

Vanessa obtained a Registered Representative license and worked at a major Wall Street investment firm. She has a Bachelor of Arts degree in Communication with a minor in Pan African Studies, a Master of Arts degree in English, and a law degree—all from the University of Louisville, in Kentucky, where she resides.

Vanessa loves the Lord more and more each day and continues to *lift* up the name of Jesus! This is her first book.